THE DEATH OF
FIDEL PÉREZ

THE DEATH OF
FIDEL PÉREZ

★

ELIZABETH HUERGO

Unbridled
Books

This is a work of fiction. The names, characters, places and incidents are either the product of the author's imagination or are used fictitiously, and any resemblance to actual persons living or dead, business establishments, events, or locales is entirely coincidental.

Unbridled Books

Copyright © 2013 by Elizabeth M. Huergo

Chapter 1, "The Moncada Army Barracks Raid," was excerpted in *Gravity Dancers: Even More Fiction by Washington Area Women* (Paycock Press, Spring 2009), ed. Richard Peabody.

Chapter 3, "Pedro Valle's Dream," was excerpted in *Full Circle: A Journal of Poetry and Prose* (Summer 2003) and reprinted in *The Best of Full Circle* (Spring 2004).

Library of Congress Cataloging-in-Publication Data

Huergo, Elizabeth.
The death of Fidel Pérez / by Elizabeth Huergo.
p. cm.
ISBN 978-1-60953-095-2
1. Cuba—Fiction. I. Title.
PS3608.U34963D43 2012
813'.6—dc23
2012037563

1 3 5 7 9 10 8 6 4 2

Book Design by SH • CV

First Printing

A Georgina Martínez Huergo,
madre, amiga fiel,
y la narradora en mi corazón

★

The Writer himself knows
that the only revolution is the permanent one—
not in the Trotskyite sense,
but in the sense of the imagination,
in which no understanding is ever completed,
but must keep breaking up and re-forming
in different combinations
if it is to spread and meet
the terrible questions of human existence.

NADINE GORDIMER,
Living in Hope and History

★

It is not the voice that commands the story:
it is the ear.

ITALO CALVINO,
Invisible Cities

CHAPTER ONE

SOME FIFTY YEARS after the 1953 Moncada Army
Barracks Raid, at nearly seven o'clock on the morning of
July 26th, and at just the moment when the sun's rays rose
magically from the edges of the earth, Fidel Pérez, who
had already ingested a quart of *Chispa de tren*, the cheap-
est beer his younger brother Rafael had found on the
black market, was nursing a badly broken heart. This
Fidel, a dissolute, angry Romeo bereft of his tatty Juliet,
stepped out onto the balcony that ran the full perimeter
of his brother's apartment to face the dawn. Lacking all
appreciation for the morning's charms, he belched loudly,
raised both fists, and furiously jabbed his middle fingers
toward the sun as if it were the miserable slut who had
betrayed him the week before. Infuriated at the sun's ambivalence, he leaned over the railing and shouted down at

the balcony two floors below his, where he knew the middle-aged Isabel must still be sleeping, her husband beside her.

"*¡Isa! ¡Isa, te amo! ¡Isa, eres mia! ¡Mia solamente!*"

The alcohol that after a week of drinking allowed him to lower his manly guard and sob openly also slurred his speech. So even Rafael, in the kitchen making coffee, his head splitting in pain, was startled by his brother's sudden patriotic fervor for the *isla*, the island with which, oddly enough, Fidel seemed so consumed that morning. Rafael had never known his brother to insist so adamantly on how much he loved the *isla*; how much the *isla* belonged to him only. Rafael was smiling, having just realized what Fidel was actually shouting about, when he heard the sound of the balcony and its rusted iron balustrade giving way.

"*¡Hijo de la gran puta!*" Fidel screamed, the hum of alcohol in his brain giving way to terror.

Rafael dropped the hot coffee and ran to the edge of the broken balcony just in time to see Fidel clinging, his fingers wrapped tightly around the balustrade, his body dangling in midair.

"*¡Socorro! ¡Fidel se calló!* Help! Fidel's fallen!" Rafael shouted.

Shocked by the fragility of life, in that moment Rafael's cry for help was both practical, an expression of his desire to save the hard-drinking older brother he loved, and incantatory, a plea cast like a magical spell, a wish that this evil fork itself onto a different path and that this terrible misfortune belong to some other Fidel.

Rafael lurched over the broken threshold and grabbed fast to his older brother's forearms. But the weight of Fidel's body was too much, or the strength of Rafael's grip too little, or the decay of the balcony too extensive.

Justicio, their neighbor directly across the street, was carefully wheeling his bicycle cab out of the communal garage on the ground floor when he heard an uncannily familiar voice shouting about his love for the island and then a horrible rending sound he couldn't identify. Justicio looked up just in time to see the Pérez boys falling, in a terrible embrace, tumbling headfirst toward the front garden that had been covered in concrete so many years earlier. He watched their bodies strike the concrete, though it took him what seemed an eternity to absorb what he had witnessed.

The Pérez boys never had a chance, Justicio thought, crossing the street, kneeling before their entangled bodies, and closing their eyes.

"*¿Que paso, Justicio?*"

"*Fidel calló—*" Justicio explained, gesturing toward the bodies and the pile of rubble on the ground.

"*¿Y este quien es?*"

"*El hermano.*"

"*¿Los dos calleron?*"

"*Fidel calló y el hermano tambien,*" Justicio said.

He knelt sorrowfully by the bodies of the two brothers, still warm, their embrace intact. He watched the neighbors who had heard the commotion flock around the bodies, craning their necks to catch a glimpse of the blood that had begun to drip down from the concrete garden and onto the sidewalk below.

"*¡Fidel! ¡Fidel! ¡Dios mio, Fidel!*"

No one stopped to consider that Isabel, the woman who had broken Fidel's heart, was addressing the pulpy remains of her latest conquest. There she stood at the center of a swirling vortex of confused people who had become strangely unaware of the brothers' mangled bodies and more interested in the spectacle of Isabel, wailing like a witch bereft of her familiar, her unkempt mane of hair trailing behind her, her arms flailing, and her ample bosom bursting from the grip of a nearly transparent bathrobe as she expressed the anguish of a very good neighbor.

The voices of the onlookers rose in empathy around the inconsolable Isabel, eventually building to a ponderous weight.

"*¡Fidel calló!*" a young man shouted from the top of a nearby lamppost that he had managed to climb with some effort.

"His brother, too," Isabel's husband echoed, his enormous, furry belly pressing through the rails of his bedroom balcony.

The crowd below them began to sway and roll under the weight of emotion.

"*¡Fidel calló!*" Isabel wept.

"His brother, too!"

"*¡Fidel calló!*"

"His brother, too!"

The Pérez brothers, known for nothing in life except the boyish charm that enabled them to cadge most of whatever they needed, now in death began to catalyze an inadvertent turn toward consciousness. The people who heard the commotion early that morning found themselves at a threshold between worlds, suspended for that last aching moment like water coalescing, loosening its tensile grip and then dropping and splattering onto a new surface, much as the body of Fidel and his brother had done.

"What a fitting day for Fidel and his brother to die," someone said.

Justicio, still kneeling by the bodies, looked up. For him, seeing the bodies of the Pérez boys tumbling to their deaths was like witnessing the deaths of his own two sons, or the death of those hopes he had once held in his heart for that generation born on the cusp of revolution. His sons and the Pérez boys—they were stunted, their intelligence yoked to the practical matter of living, of scrambling each and every day to find enough to eat, enough gasoline and parts to make whatever contraption they could get their hands on run another few kilometers. That was all they knew.

"Don't be so offended, *hombre.*" The man grinned. "You have to admit. It's funny. Of all the days of the year. This little dictator and his brother died today, July 26th."

A dark wave of laughter curled through the crowd. Justicio stood up, searching for something to say. Instead he pushed through the crowd and back across the street to the garage where he had left his bicycle cab, his mind drifting, in search of comfort or distraction, and settling unexpectedly on the long-ago image of Fulgencio Batista, his face staring out from the front page of the newspaper. After the Moncada Army Barracks Raid of 1953, Batista had Fidel arrested, tried, and convicted, but he could neither leave him to languish in a prison cell nor kill him. To the Cuban public, Fidel had become a latter-day Robin Hood. So, in order to preserve himself, Batista released Fidel and exiled him to Mexico, never expecting that in 1956 Fidel, along-side his brother Raúl and Che Guevara and seventy-nine other revolutionaries, would return in secret to Cuba. Batista never expected that the peasant farmers along the Sierra Maestra would feed and support Fidel or that the hungriest and the most outraged of the middle class would pour into the streets to welcome him.

In the years between the 1953 Moncada Army Barracks Raid and the Revolution of 1959, as Batista was losing his dictatorial grip on the island, the U.S. continued to insist publicly on its neutrality, all the while supplying Batista's government with arms and military training. In the streets of Havana and other cities and towns across Cuba, men and women were openly clubbed for opposing Batista; prison cells became torture chambers; and police officers members of death squads. The killing and maiming spiraled indiscriminately. The more Batista repressed every grassroots urge for democracy, the more the U.S.

buttressed Batista's repression and the more reasonable and noble Fidel appeared. Justicio remembered how Batista's once smug expression disappeared, replaced by the mask that stared out at him from the page: disbelieving, primal, the look of an animal startled, paralyzed by fear. He remembered the dark wave of spite and joy that washed over him; that made him one with the sardonic stranger.

"*¡Justicio! ¡Justicio! ¿Que paso?*" Irma shouted down to him frantically from an open window.

"Fidel and his brother have fallen," Justicio shouted back, not an ounce of emotion in his voice.

"*¿Donde vas?*" Irma shouted, upset that he was leaving.

Justicio made believe he hadn't heard her and began pedaling away. He didn't want to stay. There was nothing he could do. All he wanted was to leave the past, to leave calamity far behind him and to concentrate on how he would feed his family today. He didn't care that it was July 26th, he told himself. As for the sacrilegious stranger, Justicio knew he was no better.

Much like Justicio, some of the good citizens who overheard the sardonic stranger that morning were quite old, as old as the Moncada Barracks hero of 1953 they remembered so well. Gathered there in the street, fearful of change, they could still remember something that had come before this surface they had grown so accustomed to, clinging mindlessly, day after day, until the days had grown into years and the years into decades. For others in the crowd, the 1953 raid was a vague legend. They were so young that Fidel's fall today triggered only a cascade of possibilities, possibilities so enticing that there was no such thing as fear or death or unmitigated suffering. Still others were approaching middle age, and the awareness of their mortality, not as an abstraction but as something visceral, felt in the bone and sinew, had already begun to form its own critical mass, rising within them like an unrelenting tide. Whatever dreams they once had were drained away, revealing the underlying rock, the certainty that time had rendered their passivity into inadvertent choices, while the actual lives they had once imagined had been left unlived and far behind.

At that precise moment, the unexpected and indecorous joke exacerbated a breach between what they had all tacitly accepted and what they all understood and desired. Their laughter transformed each of them, young and old and in between, into conspirators who shared the same hopes. They recognized one another. The decades of being separated had passed and were beyond repair, but now the bond among them was irrevocable, the cumulative energy of their response drawing them together with a force as great as gravity, rising to an enormous crest, then shattering over their regrets.

One particular good citizen, Saturnina, was squatting on a doorstep just a few blocks away, feeding a hard biscuit to a hungry stray dog, when she heard the news that Fidel and his brother had fallen. Saturnina rose from her corolla of ragged skirts and began to walk toward the throng of people gathering before the building and spilling over into the street, blocking the morning traffic. Though she could see nothing of what had happened, in a swirl of petticoats and skirts she began to mimic the words she heard:

"*¡Socorro! ¡Fidel calló!* Help! Fidel has fallen!"

Saturnina, Sybil of the succulent bit of news that lodges like a string of pork gristle in the space between back teeth, began to fidget and whirl her way through the edges of the gathering crowd, calling out what she had instantly accepted as fact: The apocalypse that would precede the return of her son Tomás, whom she had lost decades earlier in the violent interregnum between Fulgencio Batista and Fidel Castro, had begun.

"*¡Fidel calló!* His brother has fallen, too!"

Stepping and swirling, the old woman tripped along the farthest perimeter of the bloody scene. As she passed along the streets calling out her news, housewives peered through rusted iron rails, pulling back quickly into darkened interiors. Men and women on errands or on their way to work or school stopped to listen, then sped on, looking back over their shoulders nervously.

"What did that old woman say?"

"Fidel has fallen!"

"The old man is gone?"

"Yeah, his brother, too."

"You sure?"

The news of Fidel's death began to travel like molten rock down a mountainside, obliterating everything in its path and transforming itself from liquid to solid by the time it reached the entrance to the University of Havana.

"What are they saying about that sick old man?"

"Fidel is gone!"

"What about Raúl?"

"Fidel is Fidel. Fidel can't be replaced."

"I'm telling you they're both gone."

"The government has collapsed?"

"Gone in a single stroke."

The lava swirled and eddied as it traveled down the

long avenues, oozing past statues of nineteenth-century generals and plazas spotted with bronze plaques. Spreading, the news flowed down the white marble avenues, the broken cobblestone streets, the flanks of crumbling mansions, brittle vestiges of a colonial life suspended now, like the forgotten rags hanging on frayed clotheslines attached between archways and windows.

The shocking news that Fidel and his brother had both been killed coincided with the weekly rolling blackout across parts of Havana, a practice instituted by the government to save precious electricity. Now that blackout was adding to the fear. What had become to most *Habaneros* an habitual nuisance quickly took on a foreboding quality. Fidel and his brother had fallen, and so had the city descended into a metaphorical darkness on that bright July morning.

The *Habaneros* who heard the rumors and still had electricity turned to the government radio and television stations, which that very morning had been shut down for a series of upgrades. Those upgrades had been deferred, month after month for more than a year, until the day before, when a team of Italian technicians had arrived in the city and begun to test the emergency-band frequency. So when those citizens tuned in expecting to be told that, at the very least, Raúl Castro was well, or that Fidel was fragile but holding on to life as any old man with too much power would, they heard instead a high-frequency screech, an angry bionic grasshopper, harbinger of dread and pestilence and things easily imagined by people who have nothing left in this material world.

Saturnina's cry continued to resonate along the streets, buttressing the old woman and lending her words a factual quality that belied her exhaustion. To the university students on their way to class, she seemed no more an anomaly than the mongrels that wandered from door to door or the obsolete tank on the central quadrangle of the University of Havana, Fidel's iron Rocinante, the very tank on which he had ridden into the heart of the city in 1959, only six years after the Moncada Army Barracks Raid, an event that had been dismissed at the time as a thing of no consequence, the magical thinking of puerile misfits, by the pundits who considered themselves the best sort of historians.

CHAPTER TWO

★

"¡Saturnina, Saturnina!
Vuelta das tan clandestina.
¡Saturnina, Saturnina!
Dando vueltas, ¿qué destinas?"

Saturnina struggled to walk deeper and deeper into the center of the crowd that had gathered at the spot where Fidel and his brother had fallen. She found herself swarmed by the squealing, singing children who loved her but had no inkling of the agony of her mission.

"*Tengo hambre*, Saturnina," one of the boys called out to her, rubbing his belly.

She handed out the remaining hard biscuits she kept stuffed in the pockets of an apron located many layers deep under her skirts. She gave each child a pat on the head, then continued to push through toward the center of the enormous crowd. When the press of bodies blocked her from going farther, she squatted, then crawled through a forest of legs and feet until she reached the center. She could see that the bodies had been removed. She crawled closer. She could see the pool of blood. She crawled closer. Now she could touch the blood that covered the concrete. Fidel's viscous blood, the blood of a dictator, was on her fingertips and palms. She looked at her skirts and saw that his blood had wicked upward along their frayed edges. It was an omen. She was certain of it. If the speed with which the blood had merged with the color and pattern of her skirts was any indication, then her son would be here soon. Time had folded back on itself like the wings of a dove, like the arms of her beloved boy around her. What had been done would be undone.

"*Fidel calló!*" Saturnina shouted, pulling on the pant legs closest to her, trying to get back up on her feet.

"Fidel is gone!" the nearly naked Isabel sobbed.

Still on her hands and knees, Saturnina strained to see the woman who had seen the blood and understood.

"What about Raúl?" a man standing just behind Saturnina asked.

"Fidel is Fidel. You should know that," Saturnina heard another man shout angrily.

"Fidel can't be replaced," someone else lamented.

Saturnina pulled with all her strength on a different pant leg as the voices continued to volley over her head.

"They're both gone."

"The government collapsed?"

"Fidel relapsed?"

"Hey, you! What'd that guy say?"

"*¡Fidel calló!*" Saturnina shouted.

"The government collapsed?"

"The balcony collapsed."

"They were both killed!"

"*Coño*, help me up," Saturnina shouted, fearful they would begin to stampede, disoriented by the voices around her, the reverberations of their words as ceaseless as a tide.

"What did she say?"

"Both killed in a stroke."

"They fell from the balcony."

"He had a stroke?"

"Yeah, he had a stroke and fell."

"His brother, too?"

"Raúl saw his brother die!"

"Imagine seeing that go off."

"The balcony was blown up?"

"Who blew up the balcony?"

"Maybe Raúl? He wants power."

"Raúl killed his brother!"

"Is that true?"

"That woman just said so."

"Which one?"

"The one with the great tits in the see-through robe."

"Where?"

"Here, down here. Help me," Saturnina shouted, feeling submerged, unable to breathe.

Saturnina sank the few teeth she still had into the bare, hairy calf that was closest to her. The man winced in pain and looked down.

"Shithead! Help me," Saturnina demanded.

"You bit me, you old bitch," he said.

"You're lucky she didn't bite anything else while she was down there," his friends roared, laughing, raising Saturnina up by her armpits and tossing her out toward the perimeter of the crowd.

Standing on her feet again, she couldn't see the spot where Fidel and his brother had fallen, but she could see the children who had eaten her bread and often trailed behind her like a cloud of dust. They were sitting together on the top step of a steep entryway, watching like circus spectators the antics before them. The ambulance was long gone. The crowd remained, watchful and expectant. Cars and scooters had begun to flow slowly past again, passengers craning their necks to see what had happened. Everyone stood coiled, unsure of what to do. They had heard that two brothers, one quiet, the other charismatic and long-winded, had died tragically, unexpectedly, and in midsentence on a balcony. So they waited.

"Get back! Get back!"

A neighbor stepped out of a side alley and began officiously throwing pails of water on the sidewalk to wash away the blood. The crowd began to turn and shift. Saturnina watched in horror as each arcing swath of water struck the pavement, the impact sending spatters of diluted blood into the air, each droplet like a small bouncing ball striking at the passersby. Hundreds, thousands of drops of watery blood striking the feet and calves of the congregants who had gathered there to witness Fidel's fall; who must be made conscious now of the terrible burden each bore to spread the good news: Fidel had silenced them, and he and his brother had fallen. Now her beloved son Tomás would return.

"*Fidel cayó. Fidel calló.*"

"Fidel silenced. Fidel fell."

Standing at the crowd's perimeter once again, Saturnina bellowed the words with conviction, drawing both index fingers to her lips as if she were silencing a noisy child and then extending her arms in midair. She watched the children scramble down the steep stairs, more than willing to play at this new dance of hers. She loved them and took pride in being the subject of their impromptu rhymes, the one who always shared with them whatever bit of something she had as if it were some great treasure. She was, as they teased her, their dotty *abuelita* of the streets, a perfect sort of grandmother, the kind always willing to sing and play through the heat of the long afternoons, the one who sheltered them in her lap after a beating or some other mishap: Of course they would oblige her in this game to see who could shout loudest, jump highest in glee.

"*Fidel cayó. Fidel calló.*"

"*Fidel cayó. Fidel calló.*"

The children's index fingers touched their lips, unable to control the swell of irreverent laughter. Then they jumped into the air again, arms stretched toward the skies, their feet striking the ground in unison. One big thud followed by peals of children's laughter and the excited bark of mongrels, then again and again in a game that seemed to find its own momentum: a rhythm that kept extending itself through the crowd. Hundreds of people gathered on nearby stoops and driveways and open windows began to join in, unaware that this was only a children's game, initiated by an old, mad woman who found herself standing in what appeared to be an enormous mandala, spurred on by the undefined void within themselves, a space normally filled with the invisible weight of anxiety and trepidation, its boundaries now obliterated by laughter.

"*Fidel cayó. Fidel calló.*"

"*Fidel cayó. Fidel calló.*"

The words galvanized the crowd into action, pushing them to the top of a curling crest, drawing more and more people together. The words confirmed the rumor, breaking the spell that for decades had left them inanimate, suspended in time, drawing each of them into the open air, entraining them all to the same realization, the same hope, and pushing everyone out into the streets.

"*Fidel cayó. Fidel calló.*"

"*Fidel cayó. Fidel calló.*"

Out in the early-morning air they stood unfettered, aware only of what they wanted and needed to do, individually and together. The man with the bitten calf saw Saturnina and grinned, swooping her into his arms, spinning her round and round while the children screamed in glee. Others began to imitate him, catching and spinning the women around them, faster and faster, in a frenzy of joy. Saturnina, distraught at their hilarity, extricated herself from the man's arms as quickly as she could. No matter how loudly she pleaded with all of them, she couldn't make them understand. Yes, Fidel had silenced them, and yes, he and his brother had fallen. But now her son would return. She had to make them understand. She watched the eddies of dancing neighbors swirl and break away and then form again, spinning faster before they broke apart, pulling away now into smaller clusters, walking, not dancing, moving step by step, without a clear destination, only a desire to create and reach some center. Saturnina had borne witness to the fall: She had touched the blood, and the blood had touched her, become part of her. Fidel and his brother had died.

"*Fidel cayó y Fidel calló.*"

"*Fidel cayó y Fidel calló.*"

"To the plaza!" someone shouted.

"To the plaza!" the crowd roared back.

"*¡A la Plaza de la Revolución!*" they began to chant, moving now toward the possibility they had held silently in their communal imagination for so long.

CHAPTER THREE

★

"WAKE UP, PEDRO. You're going to be late again," Sonya insisted.

Through half-opened eyes, Pedro Valle could see his wife Sonya standing over him. The light of the morning sun filtering through the shutters behind her made her glow like an angel.

"I'm awake. Go back to sleep, Sonya."

"I've been up for hours, you old fool. Are you really awake?"

"I'm awake."

"Your favorite neighbor was just at the door."

"That moron."

"He wants you to check the generator."

"He always wants something."

"He's not so bad, Pedro."

"Not so bad? The other day he buttonholed me. 'Hey, Professor, what'd Marx say about the dead and the living?' He must have practiced in front of a mirror for hours. 'You mean *the weight of the dead on the brains of the living*? I didn't know the Communist Party was scheduling meetings in our stairwell,' I told him. You should have seen the little cretin's face."

"You didn't really say that, Pedro?"

"Yes, I did," Pedro lied.

"He meant it as a compliment."

"He meant to entrap me."

"He probably read it in the paper. He knows you teach history."

"He's a cretin."

"If Carlito is such a cretin—"

"*Compañero Carlito Cretino.*"

"Pedro, *por Dios.* He's so helpful."

"He's the block spy."

"You don't know that."

"You don't know he isn't. I don't know how my wife can respect a man who wears his underwear in public."

"Pedro, be charitable. He helps me when you're not here."

"I help you. I help you all the time. I wear my underwear inside."

"You wear everything inside. Are you going to get up?"

Pedro assured her he was. When she left the room, he pushed himself out of bed. He could feel his age: the life force that moved through him, and its counterpoint, the sinew-wrapped bones and skin he had become. He dressed quickly, wanting to avoid another knock on the door from his neighbor the comrade. Pedro could hear his wife opening the balcony doors that ran along the perimeter of their apartment. He could hear the mechanical clock on the dresser loudly marking the time. It was a few minutes after seven in the morning. He unlocked the front door and shuffled down three flights of stairs in his worn slippers, a box of matches in his shirt pocket.

Near the basement stairwell of the building was the water pump. The other tenants entrusted him with its safekeeping, depending on him to turn it on in the morning and off in the evening. The ritual protected the fragile pump and its miscellany of worn, half-broken parts from the power surges that followed the intermittent blackouts across Havana. Lit match in hand, he threw the switch, but instead of the familiar shudder of the engine, he heard nothing. The power was out this morning. He switched the engine off again and made his way back up the deteriorated stairwell.

"The power's out again," he told Sonya, shuffling past her in the kitchen. "You can tell Comrade Carlito the Cretin when he knocks on the door again. Tell him it's not my fault. Tell him to call for a rally against the government. Fat chance you'd ever catch our comrade doing that."

Pedro leaned into the barrel Sonya kept in reserve in the kitchen, pulled up a bucket of water, and shuffled into the bathroom. He stripped, squatted in the curtainless bathroom tub, and splashed the cold water on himself. The night before, he had fallen asleep gazing through the slats of the balcony shutters at the starlit tropical night. Now his neck hurt. He poured the remaining water over his head. He rubbed his body with the towel, stood before the mirror, and scraped away with a razor at the stubble of gray hair on his face. Nothing seemed to take away the constriction the dream had caused in his chest. This morning, for the first time, the pain continued down his left arm, coinciding with his sense of something surging up inside him, seeping through unbidden.

"Don't be mad at me, Sonya."

"Why would I be mad?"

Pedro stood in the dining room, clean shaven and dressed, peering into the kitchen, watching his wife, his coffee cup in hand.

"I have seen in the dark night over my head rain, the rays of pure light, Beauty divine," Pedro recited the lines, all the while watching his wife smiling, her head down, focusing on the dishes in the sink.

Sonya turned, and Pedro saw the young woman he had married staring back at him.

"On the shoulders of handsome women I saw wings budding: and rising from the rubble butterflies soaring."

"You canceled."

"I don't know what you mean."

"Your appointment. It does you so much good to talk."

"With that quack?"

"He helps you with your troubles, your memories of Mario."

"I'd rather talk to Mario."

"Dr. Otero is a nice enough young man."

"Don't be so damned euphemistic, Sonya. He's not young. He's middle-aged. And he's not nice. He sits there and never says a word. But I always know what he's thinking." Pedro looked at his wife. Sonya was an old woman again. "If you think I'm crazy, go ahead and say it."

"After what you went through, if anyone has the right to be crazy, it's you, Pedro. Why don't you tell Dr. Otero his silence upsets you?"

"I don't have time for this."

"Aren't you forgetting something?" Sonya asked, pointing at the worn leather briefcase he had left the day before on the dining room table.

Pedro walked back to pick up the briefcase before moving toward the front door.

"Aren't you forgetting something?" Sonya repeated.

Pedro looked at his wife blankly.

"Your manuscript."

"It's right here." Pedro smiled, tapping the briefcase.

Sonya pursed her lips and turned away.

"I remembered my promise," Pedro said. "It's done."

"You're lying."

"I have a few more edits."

Pedro could see the tears welling up in her eyes.

"It's done," Pedro lied again.

"I don't believe you."

"You'll see."

Sonya closed the apartment door behind him. Pedro stood near the threshold, briefcase in hand, thinking that he needed to return and make amends. Instead he started down the dark, narrow stairs, carefully minding each step. Just as he was reaching the landing, Pedro was certain he heard a familiar voice.

"Mario? Are you there, my friend?" he whispered.

An apartment door opened abruptly, and Pedro felt the bright flash of a torch in his eyes.

"You get to the generator yet? There's no power. Hey, you hear me, Professor? No power."

Pedro struggled to steady his breath, barely able to contain his displeasure at seeing Carlito, in a sleeveless undershirt and boxers, the stub of a cheap cigar between his teeth.

"The power's out," Pedro said.

"I know. Why you telling me that?" Carlito stepped closer. In the darkness of the stairwell, the smell of cigar smoke and stale perspiration nearly overpowered Pedro.

"You hear me?" Carlito asked, flashing the beam of light in Pedro's face.

"I tried," Pedro stammered, shrinking away from the beam, unable to fill his lungs with air.

"What's the matter, Professor? Too old to deliver?" Carlito laughed from his belly, scratching his head with the hand that held the cigar stub.

"The power's out," Pedro repeated.

"So you say." Carlito stepped closer to Pedro, using the stub of the cigar to punctuate his words. "Did you jiggle the gizmo? The gizmo on the generator. You didn't jiggle it, did you?"

"I did everything I could," Pedro said, reaching back to find the hand rail and nearly losing his footing on the stairs.

Carlito lunged forward to catch him, the torch dropping, sounding loudly on the terrazzo floor and going dark, but Pedro pushed away in fear, shuffling down the remaining stairs as fast as he could.

"Professor, you okay?"

Pedro didn't answer. Once out on the cobblestone sidewalk, he clung to the iron gate. He couldn't name the feeling welling up inside him, folding back like a tide, striking him, each time causing every frustration, every fear he had ever felt, to rise and choke him, to demand what he couldn't give.

"Hey, Pedro—"

"I'm fine, Carlito. Do me a favor. Tell Sonya I'll finish."

"You okay?"

"Tell her. Would you tell her? I'll finish."

Pedro released his grip on the gate and stepped onto the sidewalk, leaving behind his disappointed wife and intrusive neighbor.

CHAPTER FOUR

"Saturnina sangrando vino
A decirnos el destino.
Girando viene, las sallas sangrosas.
Girando va, contando muertos como losas."

Saturnina watched the crowd coalesce and begin to make its way to the plaza. She felt the press of an invisible hand at her back, propelling her away from the commotion, pushing her across the city as if she must mark the hour of doom and salvation. She moved toward the trees in the square, toward the grass tamed into rectangles by the surrounding brick. She felt the tiny green teeth of each blade biting her ankles, pressing against her flesh. She watched as the blades of grass changed color—no longer green but turquoise, like the morning sky. She saw the drops of water from the predawn rain coagulating on the bricks before her, their shiny translucence unaltered by the tread of broken shoes. The trees in their prison rectangles stretched into the dome of morning sky and smiled at her, despite their sorrows, all the while plunging deeper into the earth and beyond their visible prison. She touched the dark-stained bark, rough-furrowed cloak that channeled the rain deeper into the roots, and looked up to see the massive limbs, jostled by the breeze, with each movement reframing segments of the sky.

"Dime," she whispered to the bark. Tell me. "Can you hear me?"

The cars sputtered along both sides of the avenue. The houses shrank imperceptibly into the soil, their movements glacier-like. Their faces reflected Saturnina's own: unshuttered, broken by time, entire pieces missing, and yet insistent. They held within themselves a series of histories, of those who had lived and died within those walls, and of those who had come here to imagine and then build them.

"When I stand here," Saturnina began to tell the tree, "I feel heaven. The Lord dangles me head down by the ankles. Then I stretch my arms out toward the world. He massages the soles of my aching feet and helps me through another day. He pulled Tomás up into the heavens and held him safely in His arms until today. Batista's men, the ones who killed Tomás, the Lord let go of their ankles long ago. The Lord sent them spinning into oblivion."

Saturnina felt the press of the invisible hand propelling her forward again. She hobbled along as quickly as her aching knees would carry her. She passed the ruined buildings, the mosaics on each façade shattered by time. She could feel the tesserae striking the ground, her heart constricting as each one began to dissolve into the dust. She felt obliged to stop and rescue as many as she could, placing them carefully in a small pouch by her side.

She liked to hear the tesserae clicking, rubbing against one another; the soft swoosh of her many skirts and the counterpoint of colorful marble. She liked to collect these pieces every day and then at nightfall empty the pouch on the floor of the broken attic she called home. She would light a candle, arrange the tesserae by color and pattern, and whisper a prayer to the God who held her ankles so delicately, that He might watch over these hardened tears that dropped from her buildings just as He watched over her son in heaven.

"*¡Fidel calló!*" Saturnina cried out to every passerby.

She walked as fast as she could, surveying the ground before her, picking up bits of fallen marble, trying to ignore the smell of fried dough in the air and the growl it had triggered in her belly. She had given away her last bit of bread to the children, and she wondered if there would be bread today at the food dispensary. The pouch of tesserae jostled on her hip, the sugary dough sizzled in the morning air, the invisible hand pressed against her back. She didn't have a single *centavo* in that pouch, so if the dispensary was closed, she would have to wander back with an even emptier belly into the heart of the city. She would have to stop by the farmers' market stalls and find a soul who would take pity and give her a handful of uncooked beans or a ripe mango.

The old woman covered her face and began to cry. The press of that invisible hand pushed her forward, the undertow of sorrow and regret pulled her under, until her mind began tumbling through the past, the image of her broken son on an aluminum slab at the city morgue rising before her. She felt the stiffened hands that had once held hers, tiny fingers wrapping round her immortal soul. All the fighting and the blood and the words—her son had been taken away unjustly, but he would return.

"*¡Tomás! ¡Tomás! ¿No quieres café?*"

"*No, Mamá,*" she could still hear him saying. "I'll have some of your lovely coffee later."

The sound of Tomás's voice was so close by today that

it was nearly unbearable. His voice had become amplified, as if all at once Tomás had become many people and was shouting at her from many different directions.

"*¡Tomás! ¡Tomás! ¡Fidel calló!*"

Each time she called out the day's news to him, Tomás shouted back, the sound reverberating in her head, confusing her. Why was her boy shouting at her? This beloved son whose whispers she usually strained to hear, his voice like the rustle of new leaves in a summer breeze, today was shouting at her as loudly as a gale wind across bare-limbed trees.

"*Madrecita, viejita de mi alma,*" the first soldier called out to Saturnina as she approached the dispensary. "*Aquí tienes pan.*"

"Comrade, take your bread!" the second soldier barked.

Saturnina grasped the small loaf, tucking it inside her blouse.

"No lines today," the first soldier said, shrugging, a crooked smile on his face. "Why don't you take these, too? No one's here."

Saturnina said nothing but held out her skirts to receive the few hard biscuits that remained on the dispensary shelf, receiving them as if she were waiting for communion—a pragmatic, unexpected communion held before a ramshackle wooden shed and dispensed by a couple of priests in army fatigues.

"*Fidel calló,*" Saturnina explained, offering them the words in gratitude.

"*Madrecita—*" the soldier with the crooked smile began. Saturnina saw him raise a forefinger to his lips. "Be careful."

Saturnina gave him a sidelong glance, her ancient underlip jutting into the infinity of space before her, the rope of her hair twisted into a crown at the top of her head. She looked down and remembered the bloody edges of her skirts. She wasn't certain which frightened her more, the knowledge she carried with her or the smiling soldier's response to her words.

"*Calló. Fidel calló. ¿Qué van hacer?*" Saturnina asked softly, calmly.

"Get out of here," the second soldier commanded. "You're lucky I'm not arresting you, you crazy old loon. Fidel is alive."

"*Fidel calló.* What will you do? Who will you stand with?" Saturnina insisted.

"Do what he says. Don't come back again, *madrecita.* For your own good," the soldier with the crooked smile insisted.

Saturnina squinted. Why did he insist on calling her *madrecita?*

"¿Tomás?"

The soldier with the crooked smile shook his head.

"José," he offered.

"I understand," Saturnina replied, winking.

Saturnina lifted the uppermost layers of her skirts until she reached the old apron with the deep pockets. She stuffed the hard biscuits into her pockets, then pulled the small loaf from her blouse and took a bite.

"You remind me of my mother," José said.

"I am your mother, boy. You all belong to me."

She smacked her lips and cocked her left eyebrow.

"Remember," Saturnina said, shaking an arthritic forefinger at him, "I was the one. I told you the truth. What are you going to do? Who will you stand with? You'll have to decide."

The second soldier scowled at her. Saturnina turned and walked a short distance from the dispensary.

"*¡Fidel callo!* You'll have to decide. Soon."

Saturnina scurried away, shrugging off the volley of curses the second soldier hurled at her. She began the walk back to her hovel. As she walked, she broke off small pieces of bread, putting each piece in her mouth, chewing and walking until she reached the ruin she called home. From the outside it appeared intact, the blue-and-white Alhambra tiles that decorated the façade and entrance untouched. Inside, most of the walls and ceilings had collapsed onto the ground floor, slowly, piece by piece, covering in rubble the marble surface of the once grand foyer. Only the top floor, the carved wooden stairs, and a portion of the roof that extended precariously over the rubble remained. It was here, in this niche that extended from the landing and along one of the interior walls, that she made her home. She climbed up the long, rickety staircase and sat on the top landing in her battered rocker, glancing up at the morning sky through the broken walls of the building and then down at the passersby flitting across the broad entranceway below her.

Fidel's death had triggered in her a set of barely dormant preoccupations that began now to shift and commingle with the sound of the children's rhymes floating across from the building behind hers. She thought about how much she liked to play with the children; how they would call out their rhymes, running at her full tilt, fearless, like birds in flight. They trusted her dusty lap and her arthritic hands, which even now, in old age, could grip and raise them toward the sky. They would dance circles around her, hiding in the folds of her skirt, laughing from their hard, round bellies at the old woman, old as a rock, dark as a river idol raised from the mysterious depths on a fisherman's hook.

They were her children, she thought. Even the soldiers were hers. She extended her right hand before her proprietarily, beneficently, as if she were blessing her congregants. These were Saturnina's streets, her cobblestones under the tropical sun, her bony mongrels that sniffed and scraped for any morsel and died among thick cords of flies, their rib cages thrust into the midday air, defiant. The streets that tilted down in a long cascade, eventually finding their way to the sea; these were hers. The rusted wrought-iron balustrades; the perilously worn balconies; the toothless slatterns who hung their dingy laundry across rows of drooping rope suspended between doorways; these belonged to her, too. Sorrowful Saturnina, her neighbors called her, harmless bag of bone and flesh buffeted by forces so much greater than herself; crazy old woman, living trough of memory and despair. How she liked to rock back and forth on her perch every day and think about Tomás, her sweet and only boy, calling out his name.

"¡Tomás! ¡Tomás!"

She rocked steadily back and forth, calling out to him as if he were in the next room, as if he would be bringing her a bag of yarn, a misplaced pair of glasses. But today only the image of Tomás's bloodied body and that last, startled look on his face rose before her.

Though Saturnina lived through the turmoil at the end of Batista's regime and the beginning of Fidel's, she remembered very little, images of the violence and injustice of those years imprinting themselves on her memory as if they had been observed by someone else. She moved through the days and months after Tomás's death practically, methodically—the way someone moves through a series of facts memorized but not quite understood. She had always known about Tomás's interest in politics; she had never realized how actively he had been working against Batista, joining the Revolutionary Directorate and running an underground student network that provided food and shelter for dissenters of every political stripe. He had been arrested several times, but so had many of the university students who were members of the Directorate, and who had sworn themselves to the overthrow of Batista.

Saturnina remembered asking Tomás's classmate, Armando, to tell her what had happened.

"They singled him out. They singled a lot of us out," Armando explained. "They saw Tomás as part of the Directorate's conspiracy to assassinate Batista."

"Was he?"

"I don't know, Saturnina."

"You must know, Armando. You were with him."

"I just helped him shelter dissenters. We never told one another anything that could be used against us."

"He sheltered people, Armando. He would never kill."

"He never turned anyone away. Maybe he should have."

"He sheltered people."

"He sheltered dissenters. That was enough to get him killed, but I don't know."

"Who killed him, Armando?"

"I saw the American pull the trigger. I saw him," Armando explained. "I don't know who hired him or why."

Even now Saturnina tried to imagine the moment when the American with the thin mustache had called out her son's name, Tomás Olivera Díaz, and how Tomás had stepped forward, with that frankness that was intrinsic to his character, and discovered a cocked revolver. Not a single friend standing on the dock with Tomás that day could explain to Saturnina what had happened to the American, who seemed to have been absorbed by the chaos that followed. She knew with an abiding faith that her son, in his last flicker of consciousness, had recognized and forgiven him. The boy who helped everyone the way she had taught him would have forgiven this, too. She imagined the American, lit cigarette in hand, standing in a far corner of the dark interrogation room that last time Tomás had been arrested by Batista's men and then abruptly released.

"They didn't want to kill him there," Armando explained.

"But they did kill him, didn't they?" Saturnina asked.

"Yes, Saturnina."

"Are you sure, Armando?"

"Yes."

"Are you sure he's dead?"

"Yes, Saturnina."

"But why, Armando?"

"I don't know, Saturnina."

At her insistence, Armando recounted to her over and over again the details of what had happened until Saturnina could imagine the burnished revolver's soft gleam, smell the acrid cloud of powder expanding through the air, and feel the pressure of the stranger's finger on the trigger. Armando told her the story of her son's assassination, and with each retelling the details would reverberate within Saturnina, heaving, fading, reconstituting themselves within the ebb and flow of her obsessive desire to witness Tomás's last breath, as she had witnessed his first. She had gone to the city morgue with his wife Vania and his friend Armando to identify his body, but she had never been able to reconcile the son she loved and raised with the body lying on that table, the flesh of her son's face as hard and cold as its metal surface.

"This is not my son. I don't know who this is."

"It is," Armando and Vania explained.

"¡*Tomás! ¡Tomás!*" Saturnina called out now, as she had that day in the morgue.

The fragments of Armando's story, so difficult to accept, began to dance across the shifting surface of her mind, hurtling her backward and forward through time, until eventually she began to insist to Vania, Tomas's young widow, that Tomás would rise, like Lazarus, awakening to this world again.

"This son of mine will come back," she insisted.

In 1959, still nursing the terrible wound of Tomás's death, she and Vania poured into the streets of Havana along with every race and class of Cuban. They were celebrating the end of Batista and the arrival of Fidel—

El Caballo, the Horse—who had descended from the Sierra Maestra like an avenging angel in green army fatigues and a long beard to liberate them all from Batista's puppet government, a regime whose brutality had been sanctified and financed by the United States. That very week Saturnina played *charadas*, but instead of putting her *peso* down on number 17, Lazarus, the beloved whom Christ raised from the dead, her favorite saint since Tomás's death, she played the number 1, the Horse.

"Saint Lazarus won. Paid 50 *pesos*."

She had spent countless hours explaining this irony of fate to her favorite mongrel, who rocked behind her on three legs, his white coat gray with fleas.

"Saint Lazarus," she would intone, her left eyebrow cocked meaningfully. "Not the Horse."

It was a bad omen. The Horse was not what he seemed. He would delay the arrival of Lazarus. Saturnina was certain. Fidel would not liberate them. He would be their torment, just as Batista had been. Saturnina remembered crying out to the skies, hoping her words would reach Tomás:

"You died fighting Batista. This *puñetero* Fidel is the same."

Today, however, something had shifted. She knew it.

Rocking back and forth on her stairwell perch, she could see that the morning sky held new auguries. The bad omen of '59 had been undone. The Horse was gone. The promise of Saint Lazarus had come to pass. The tears rolled down Saturnina's ancient face. She had waited for what seemed an eternity, but her faith had been rewarded. Christ would raise Tomás. She had prayed, believing; and believing, she knew. Tomás would be back soon.

The sound of a trumpet blaring in the distance startled her. From the top of the broken stairwell, she looked down through the gauzy scrim of her cataracts at the entranceway far below and noticed an odd figure hovering there, glowing as white as the flesh of a coconut, his countenance aggrieved. It was the angel of the annunciation. She was certain of it.

"*Pobresito,*" Saturnina whispered, trying to imagine the angel's burden. "I will do as you command. Don't be sad."

There was no time to dawdle. She must spread the message: Fidel had fallen, and her son Tomás would be here soon. She must tell La Milagrosa, one grieving mother to another.

him, blustering through the house as if her husband's laments could be shooed away like chickens.

Justicio hadn't heard her. He was biting into his dry morning biscuit and drinking his cup of *café con leche* to the dregs, recalling his old two-door Chevy Del Ray. When at last the car could offer nothing except worn parts to be sold on the black market, that's what he did: He sold them—carburetor, tires, spark plugs, steering wheel, mirrors, belts. Whatever had not disintegrated with use, Justicio sold bit by bit, eventually using the money to buy another vehicle, a Schwinn Spitfire with a two-seater cab welded to the back, a contraption composed of aluminum tubes and patched wicker and a canvas top with yellow and red stripes, long faded, and a tattered fringe, once bright white, that ran along its edges.

God has His ways, Justicio thought. He remembered looking down into his empty cup and hearing Irma on the rear balcony beating the bedroom rug mercilessly, his wife's way of expressing the inexpressible. Justicio smiled to himself, recalling the moment. We are given everything we need. The bicycle cab had allowed him to make a living for himself, Irma, and their two sons. He had been given a chance and decided to place his faith in the muscular strength God had given him and a plastic-covered image of the most charitable Virgen del Cobre. *La Virgensita,* the patroness of Cuba, had appeared to three desperate men from Cayo Francés, two native Indians and an African slave, who found themselves cast one day upon a turbulent sea in a fragile dinghy. Justicio wasn't sure why the three men were in the dinghy. He had forgotten that part of the story, but he knew that before the Virgin appeared in the sky, that dinghy was all they had.

Having nothing and then experiencing the good fortune of finding and purchasing the bicycle cab, Justicio had dedicated it to the Virgin, placing her image in an old plastic sleeve and hanging it from the small rearview mirror. That bicycle cab fed his hungry family for many years, including the leanest years of the U.S. embargo. After the birth of his second grandchild, deformed by malnutrition, his faith again began to falter. So he punched a small hole through the plastic's bottom edge and tied a string of brass bells to it. Every time his wheels struck a rough patch in the road, the bells would jangle and remind him of the Virgin and the common bond between himself and the poorest of the poor, the two native Indians and the slave, who centuries earlier had witnessed her appearance in the sky.

"Did you finally kill the rug?" Justicio remembered

asking his wife when she bustled into the room again, carrying a pail of water and a mop.

"I'm going to kill you if you don't get out of my way, funny guy," Irma warned him.

"You'd miss me, Irma."

Justicio rose from his chair and helped her with the heavy pail, planting a kiss on her mouth.

"Don't be fresh, old man."

"I'm never stale."

"You're dirtier than this floor. When are you going to stop pedaling that cab? It's too much for you. You're too old."

"I'll see you later. Don't you do too much, Irma."

Irma didn't want him to continue doing such a physically demanding job as he got older, but Justicio insisted that he knew his limits, selected his tourists and occasional natives with great care, ignoring anyone with voluminous buttocks or belly or too many packages who tried to wave him down. In fact, though the wicker-and-canvas cab seated two, these days he normally only picked up one passenger at a time. Slim-hipped girls with only a simple handbag, he told Irma; the rounder and smaller their buttocks the better, he always added, grinning, knowing the comment would cause Irma to roll her eyes and call him a dirty old goat, which in turn made him howl with laughter.

He was wheeling the bicycle cab out of the communal garage on the ground floor when he heard a familiar voice shouting about his love for the island and then a horrible rending sound he couldn't identify. Justicio looked up just in time to see the Pérez boys falling, their bodies striking the concrete. He struggled to make sense of what he had witnessed, to cross the street and tend to their terrible wounds, and when he could do no more, to close their eyes and whisper under his breath the only bits of the extreme unction he remembered.

Justicio fretted. For some reason, he had been cast down into troubled waters. He began pedaling as fast as he could, glancing every now and then at the face of the Virgin, who appeared to him today inscrutable and aloof. The bells shook and jangled, but the sound brought him only an unbearable sense of life's fragility. What had happened to the Pérez boys could happen to his own sons; an entire generation had been stunted. The absentminded Justicio let the front wheel of his bicycle cab scrape against the curb as he slowed down to make a right-hand turn.

The Virgin jangled her approval. The brothers' tragic deaths, he thought; why had he been made to witness such a sight? It must all have a higher purpose. The Virgin jangled her approval with even greater energy as Justicio, paying less attention to the road than he should as he pedaled his way toward El Vedado, let the front wheel of his bicycle cab dive into an enormous pothole. The most hopeful thing he could do was to keep to his usual routine, riding through El Vedado, then out to El Parque de los Martires later in the day, having something to eat, and taking a short nap on one of the park benches before pedaling along the avenue that flanked El Malecón, looking for that last wave of weary tourists in need of a ride back to the Hotel Nacional.

The rim of the sun's disc had barely broken through the inky plumes of clouds, residue of the late-night rain, as Justicio reached the intersection of Calle J and Avenida 17.

He pedaled past a middle-aged woman, her hair the color of brass, stooping over her buckets of white *azucenas*, carefully arranged on the sidewalk, the sweet scent of the flowers hanging in the air. He smiled and waved at the sleepy workers leaning against the trunks of the royal palms, their thumbs extended, waiting for the Samaritan who might give them a lift and save them the crush of public transport. He heard the cars roaring by, farcical, balletic, along the now asphalt-covered trajectories that had been laid hundreds of years earlier, their broken tail-pipes thundering, spewing violet-blue smoke and gasoline vapors. Fierce, defiant, they seemed to hurtle through the air unaware of mechanical limits.

On the corner of Calle L and Avenida 23, Justicio stopped, his attention drawn to the diminutive figure of an old man standing before the statue of Quijote de América. Justicio heard the grate and rumble of skateboards on concrete and turned in time to see a raggedy band of boys flying along the marble surface of the rotunda, using its surface as a network of ramps and obstacles.

"Watch out! Hey! Hey!"

"Watch out, old man!"

"Move!"

"You're in the way."

The old man gripped his briefcase tightly and tried to get out of the way, tripping and stumbling to the ground instead.

"Why didn't you move?" asked a lanky boy, his hair shellacked into a single point at the top of his head.

The boys stopped. Two of them seemed to be trying to help the old man to his feet.

"Don't hurt me," the old man cried, clutching the briefcase.

"What's he babbling about?" the lanky boy asked.

"Who cares?" another boy said, tapping his skateboard impatiently against the sidewalk. "We don't have time. Whatever's going on'll be over."

"Please, don't hurt me," the old man pleaded.

A short muscular boy, his long curly hair pushed back off his forehead by a red headband, stood the old man on his feet and brushed him off.

"We have to go," the boy with the red headband explained.

"Please. I didn't mean anything," the old man said.

"Come on," the lanky one insisted.

Justicio watched the boys roll away noisily and decided to approach the old man himself.

"They're young." Justicio smiled, shrugging.

"I was young," the old man retorted. "I never wore my hair in a point like a dunce. Never wore a red headband, like a girl."

"We're all sinners. Can you walk?"

"I'm fine," the old man said, methodically brushing off

his clothes. "I have to go. I have work to do," he added, the expression on his face suggesting he had just noticed Justicio for the very first time.

"What if something else happens?" Justicio asked. "You heard the boys. Off to see what's going on."

Justicio could see a question flash across the old man's face. Instead of asking, the old man began to turn away.

"I'm Justicio."

"Pedro Valle."

"We're going in the same direction. Can I come along?"

"Suit yourself." Pedro shrugged.

Justicio walked along the street, the bicycle cab on his left, while Pedro, on his right, walked on the sidewalk. The brass bells hanging from the rearview mirror of the bicycle cab jangled in the breeze.

"What were you doing? In front of the statue, I mean," Justicio ventured.

Pedro stopped, and Justicio could feel the old man's withering stare.

"Has Quijote become an enemy of the state?"

"I was just making conversation."

Pedro nodded, but Justicio could sense the old man's persistent suspicion, his quick and now unwavering judgment of Justicio.

"When I was a boy," Pedro said, "during the Depression, my family moved from the town of Remedios, in the province of Las Villas, to Havana. We moved into a four-story apartment building just a few blocks away from here. We all had to work. Even my youngest brother, Antonio. He would sit quietly at our mother's knees and hand her the pieces of cloth she sewed together into shirts and smocks. It was my job to go out and sell each piece for a few *centavos*."

"My mother took in laundry," Justicio offered. "I helped her."

"In Remedios my father would take us all to El Parque Republicano, a rectangular park near the church, in the center of town. The park was bisected with diagonal paths that all radiated from a central gazebo. The place was filled with trees and shrubs and statues. Everyone met there at day's end. Old people would sit on wooden benches along the perimeter. Children would swarm like insects, running along the paths. Young girls would saunter by in clusters of three and four, always pretending not to see the boys around them. Couples would go there to court, strolling by arm in arm. After they were married for a while, you would see them there, trying to get away from one another."

"It was so different then," Justicio said. "I was telling my wife Irma this morning. 'If our boys had jobs,' I told her, 'they would have ambition. They would marry and build families the way our generation did. They wouldn't drink all the time.' Before the fall—"

"Before the fall?"

Justicio paused. He could see that the old man walking beside him had become agitated again.

"What do you do?" Justicio asked.

"You're one of those religious fanatics, aren't you?" Pedro ventured. "The absolute corruption of man in his fallen state? And redemption, redemption and forgiveness dangling there, impossible, some endless longing for what can't quite ever happen, not with any certainty."

Pedro paused. "I teach history, at the university."

Justicio could see his face softening, awash in a sadness that was palpable.

"My mother's faith was unshakable—and my wife, Sonya's. I've never seen anything so beautiful as their faces transfixed in prayer."

"But not you, Professor?" Justicio asked.

"I fell into history. The first time I saw the statue of Quijote de América, my father placed his hands on my shoulders. The statue and my father's hands became inextricable.

Every time my father brought me here, he would tell me stories about Spain and the immigration of his parents to Cuba. '¿*Que veremos hoy?*' he would ask. It was as if for him the history of Spain could not be told but only seen. My father's stories were like a stream of images, like the flickering movie reels in the smoky downtown theater where my brother Antonio and I would go."

"My father died when I was still a child. My mother raised all five of us by herself. I helped her. We all did."

"I'm sorry," Pedro offered.

"It was a long time ago."

Justicio felt one of the rear wheels of his cab dip into a pothole. The brass bells jangled. He looked around, aware that he had followed Pedro into the oldest part of El Vedado. It saddened Justicio to see how the neighborhood was crumbling palpably into ruin. Time had scooped out the insides of the old mansions, the way he would scoop the yolk of an egg, on those rare occasions when he could get an egg.

"Good-bye, Justicio. No need to worry about saving me," Pedro said, extending his right hand in thanks.

"Good-bye, Pedro."

Justicio lingered, unsure why he felt so solicitous toward a complete stranger. He watched Pedro Valle pass by an archway decorated with blue-and-white Alhambra tiles, pause, and glance inside as if he were peering into an ancient grotto. A wave of tenderness nearly overcame Justicio, who was certain now that he was watching a part of himself, watching some terrible dance among those who had sunk into the waters of damnation, those who had been saved, and those who clung mightily to the sides of their dinghy—waiting, hoping.

CHAPTER SIX

PEDRO VALLE LOOKED through the building's arch-way, the blue-and-white Alhambra tiles of which re-mained intact. He looked up and squinted, startled to see an old woman dressed in colorful rags sitting on a wooden rocker at the head of a winding staircase, balustrade long gone. She sat cocooned against the broken wall to her right, the canopy of turquoise morning sky visible through the crumbling plaster, the sun's rays splaying fan-like around her. He looked up at the very moment she turned to look down at him from her perch, the skin on her face stretched tight over bone and cartilage. He was held there for a moment, at the edge of an imploding grotto, head arched upward, aware of being pulled magnetically toward the old woman as if she were his moon. Then the sound of a trumpet blared in the distance, and he withdrew his gaze, embarrassed, sensing that he had intruded on the old *mulatta*.

"*Pobresita,*" Pedro whispered under his breath. Poor thing, sitting there, her dignity wrapped in those endless layers of clothes.

It was almost eight o'clock when he turned left onto Calle 27 de Noviembre, named in honor of the medical students who had been set before a firing squad on November 27, 1871, accused by the Spanish colonial authority of having vandalized the tomb of General Don Castañón. Death by firing squad, Pedro thought, inadvertently flinching, his shoulders rising to shield his head, unsure whether the popping sound he heard in the distance was an engine backfiring or something else. Feeling disoriented by the quivering din of sirens and raised voices, he pushed away from the curbstone, thrust his head and chest forward defiantly before letting them sink again, then walked the short distance to his campus office, his eyes intent on the ground before him.

Pedro reached his office door, unlocked it, and walked in, dropping his briefcase on the desk near the window. He approached the windowsill and tried to make himself look down the long cascade of white marble stairs that ran from the main quadrangle and into the city. If he let go of the sill, he would tumble headfirst onto the riverbed of marble-and-cobblestone streets and into the sea. He was certain of it. Mario had told him once that vertigo was not the fear of heights but the fear of letting go, of facing the desire to obliterate oneself.

Pedro defiantly leaned over the sill, sensing the change in his heartbeat, the adrenaline beginning to engorge the arteries along his neck as he imagined himself tumbling through space, backward down that long abyss that led to the sea. He thought of Mario, his mutilated body thrown down some remote ravine, or fed to the sharks, or dropped, still partly conscious, into a mass grave at Colón Cemetery, in a strip of land used by the Interior Ministry for the disposal of political prisoners.

Three hard taps against the frosted glass of the office door plunged Pedro deeper into the darkness of his reverie, causing him to lose his sense of time and place. He braced himself, crouching as low as he could between the window and his desk.

"Class is canceled today, Professor Valle."

The smell of stale perspiration overwhelmed Pedro. He couldn't move. He couldn't be certain whose voice he was hearing.

"Class canceled—permanently," the soldier said, smiling, tapping his baton against the left side of Pedro's neck. Tap, tap, tap—sounding the depth of Pedro's fear.

The soldiers, part of Fidel's militia, began to gut the apartment, shredding pillows and mattresses with their bayonets, skewering the clothes hanging in the closets, shattering picture frames and glass cabinets, peeling the covers from his books, spilling the contents of every drawer into a pile on the living room floor. They barked at him that he was being arrested for counterrevolutionary activities against the state and dragged him down the apartment stairwell. They took him to La Cabaña, the political prison in the old Spanish castle in the port of Havana, where they stripped him naked and threw him into a darkness so complete he lost all sense of time.

He sat bound to a chair, falling asleep every few minutes, waking to find a new set of eyes screaming the same questions at him about Mario, his whereabouts, the plots the university students and their professors had fomented against Fidel. They beat him with the blunt ends of their rifles, with rubber truncheons; they poured water into his lungs, then put him in a cell and forgot him for more than three years.

His body lacerated and swollen, Pedro was eventually slated for transport to the maximum-security prison on Isla de Pinos, far from his family, the anonymity of his death ensured. One night he was herded into a National Institute of Agrarian Reform van that lurched its way through tunnels and streets before making an unexpected stop. A pair of hands lifted up what remained of Pedro, dropping him roughly on the pavement, heavy boots kicking him unconscious again. He had been released by chance, and it was by chance that Jorge the baker came upon him the following morning, lying crumpled on a sidewalk near the corner of Dragones and Aguila, encased in the thick carapace of blood and excrement that had formed over his body. The burly Jorge threw Pedro over his shoulder like a half-empty sack of flour and carried him to a nearby clinic.

Another round of taps, louder, more insistent, roused Pedro to the present.

"Professor Valle? Are you there, Professor? It's Camilo."

Pedro had pressed himself tightly against the wall, protecting himself as best as he could against what he believed was the young officer from years ago who was about to break his jaw. He looked up to find one of his students addressing him politely, formally, embarrassed at having nudged open the door.

"Did you fall?"

"Don't hurt me."

"It's me," the student explained, helping Pedro to his feet.

"Camilo?"

"Didn't you hear me knocking?"

"I dropped something," Pedro lied.

"You told me to meet you here today. Did I get the day wrong? Everyone's out in the street. They're saying Fidel and his brother are dead."

The old man paused, uncertain how to respond. Who was *everyone*? Pedro sensed Camilo was an earnest young man. He also knew it was foolish to trust anyone. He and Sonya still closed the interior balcony windows and lowered their voices whenever the conversation shifted toward dangerous subjects.

"I was about to leave you a note," Camilo said.

Pedro held on to the windowsill and looked down at the students milling about the quadrangle. He could see the insinuation, the sudden obtrusion of something that would settle momentarily in their midst before springing to disperse again, a dark green floor of undulating sea anemones, their lips rolling in time to the rhythm of an invisible disgorgement. Seen from a distance, their movements had a fluidity and an order that struck him as both odd and comforting at the same time.

"The broadcast stations are all down," Camilo said.

Still distracted, Pedro looked at Camilo but could manage to see only himself and the trajectory of a life that extended like a broken footbridge over a precipice.

"It's probably nothing."

"They say Fidel and Raúl are gone."

"Gone where?"

"Dead."

"Who's saying that?"

"Down in the quad."

"Don't let yourself be misled by rumors, Camilo."

"Don't you believe political change is possible?" Camilo asked.

Pedro looked at Camilo and thought of Mario, who, through the brutality of Batista's regime and the chaotic rise of Fidel, had continued to believe exactly this, that real political change is possible. Mario had become a flake of ash, a lump of flesh long dissolved into a lime-spattered ditch.

"They sent you to spy on me," Pedro said. "Don't think I don't know. Don't lie to me, boy."

"Why would you think that, Professor?"

Pedro hesitated, looking at Camilo as if he were seeing him for the very first time. He didn't know anything about him except that he came to every class. The boy never took notes, yet his attention was so focused that Pedro, as he was lecturing, often felt he was speaking only to Camilo. Looking into his eyes now, Pedro could see that he had hurt the boy, that the boy was genuine. An unusual calm spread over Pedro. The decades had passed. The beatings were done. He had come out on the other side of detention.

"I had a friend, Mario, a long time ago," Pedro offered. "He used to say all good things are possible."

"What happened?"

"He was killed."

"I'm sorry."

"You remind me of him. Sometimes."

"How did he die?"

"He was disappeared."

"Is that why you don't believe political change is possible?"

"It's possible." Pedro nodded. "But you have to be willing to stake your life. You have to know, in your bones, that your sacrifice will probably mean nothing."

"It doesn't look violent down there."

"Never confuse enthusiasm with anything that could kill you."

Pedro turned away from the window. He had spoken too sternly. Someone had probably stolen something dear—a bicycle, a portable generator, a few liters of gasoline. Someone perhaps had murdered someone else in a fit of sexual jealousy or in passionate redress of a long-standing feud between brothers. The crime had drawn the crowds, and the same power outage that had kept the building's generator from working that morning had shut down the broadcast stations. These were the coincidences that had coalesced into the rumor Camilo had innocently repeated to him.

"For a short interval of time," the professor spoke to the room, "Mario convinced me. He imagined a grassroots revolution, a peaceful transformation that confronted nothing, opposed nothing. He half joked about his ideas, called them '*El Manifesto de Goya.*' Mario loved Goya. Considered him a revolutionary. Goya never confessed, he told me."

Pedro turned and saw that Camilo was listening intently.

"Goya's purpose wasn't to confess. It was to bear witness, and it became a way of seeing—and teaching. Mario was on the art department faculty and a well-known painter. As Batista's regime was uncoiling, I kept telling him how dangerous it was to define an intellectual as someone who bears witness. 'It's always dangerous to know and to speak,' he said. 'Are students here meant to learn to think or to learn their role as part of an elite class?'" Pedro smiled and fell silent. "That was Mario." He sat down heavily at his desk. "You're here to talk about your paper. Tell me again, which topic did you pick?"

Within the sound of the chanting crowd below, Pedro could hear Mario's laughter, He could still see his old friend, right leg slung over the side of one of the armchairs, staring at him with his enormous cat eyes.

"Not there, Camilo. Take the other chair. That one's broken," Pedro lied. "Which topic?"

"The Moncada Army Barracks Raid of '53," Camilo repeated. "Appropriate today."

Pedro frowned and glanced at the small calendar he had propped up against his desk lamp.

"It's July 26th."

"So it is," Pedro said.

"Would that be a good place to start, Professor Valle?"

"What?"

"The relationship between Batista and Truman?"

"Are you writing about the Raid?"

"I am," Camilo said.

"Eisenhower," Pedro corrected him. "Focus on Eisenhower. Why are you taking this class?"

"I didn't realize how much I like history," Camilo said.

"Maybe you hate agricultural engineering more, especially when it's mandated by the state."

"No," Camilo stammered. "History means everything. I mean, it helps me understand something larger than my own life."

"Terrible idea to make education 'practical'—as if all that matters in life is economics. The point is to be a moral witness, not a technician—or an apparatchik, of whatever political stripe."

"Is that what your friend said, the one who was disappeared?" Camilo asked.

"It's what I wrote," Pedro said. "Mario never wrote anything down. All these years later . . ." Pedro stopped. "I've been taking dictation from the dead." He pulled the manuscript toward him.

"I'd like to read that—if it's okay, I mean."

"At some point." Pedro nodded. "I told my wife I'd finish today."

Pedro rose from his chair brusquely, panicking at the thought of his promise to Sonya. He could tell Camilo was disappointed at being shooed out of the office, but he had work to do and fences to mend with his wife. Once Camilo left, Pedro quietly locked the door and sat down at his desk.

"Why did you tell the boy the armchair was broken?"

Pedro looked at his friend, trying to read his demeanor. There Mario sat, his elegant fingers passing a lit cigarette from one hand to the other, the smoke streaming from his nose and mouth. Pedro looked down at his own thickly veined hands, at the skin mottled with liver spots. He let his awareness settle on the ache in his lower back and knees and felt irrationally envious of Mario's youth. Mario was as young now as he had been in 1961, the day Pedro had last seen him in the café.

"It's your chair, Mario."

"You're a chronic liar," Mario said, laughing from his belly. "Pedro, come down into the streets with me. You need to see the insurgency that never dies, the one in the human breast."

"I have work to do. I promised Sonya."

"Beautiful Sonya. You finally got her."

"You died."

Pedro heard loud staccato cracks down below on the quad. He could hear the feral roar of a crowd, then a woman screaming, but he couldn't distinguish whether the sounds expressed anguish or joy. The chants of the crowd began to echo the rhythm of the truncheon from long ago. The sounds pressed against his body like a dark, water-soaked blanket until he could barely breathe. Pedro shrank into himself. He wanted to retract the perimeter of his skin deep into some untouchable core and then remain that way, inert and invisible, until the danger passed, until the selection of men for execution had been completed for the night.

Pedro could feel the wet stone floor under the piece of cardboard another prisoner had given him. The other prisoners' bodies pressed against his own, forming a mosaic of human flesh, emaciated, stricken with fear. The prisoners could see nothing from the narrow, tunnel-shaped galleries where they lay in the dark, but the dense stone of the ancient Spanish fortress resonated, magnifying every sound. From his fetal position on the floor, he could hear the scrape and fall of the soldiers' footsteps; the rusty bellow of iron doors; the cries of the political prisoner who was being dragged along the corridor, cursing, vomiting; the smell of excrement emptied by the force of fear. Then the deadly sequence of sounds would begin: the sergeant's first bellow; the crack of metal knuckles; the roar of the prisoner's last words, anguished, defiant; the sergeant's bellow; and then the most monstrous sound of all, the one that haunted Pedro's imagination: the whisper of the prisoner's last breath as each bullet struck and then expanded into the organs of his body.

Lying on the damp stone floor, Pedro could feel even the superficial wounds, inches of flesh scraped off the bone and spattered, viscous clots of paint, on the stone wall behind the pole. In the morning, the prisoners would all watch the ravens in the courtyard. Come to eat their penance, some of them would joke, insisting that the birds' feathers became darker with each passing day. The terrible nocturne continued to pierce its claws into Pedro's flesh, its enormous wings pushing the putrid air into his nose and mouth. Over and over it would resound in his head, confounding the line between wakefulness and sleep, so that his time at La Cabaña became an eternity. Naked, hungry, wounded, there was no place he could go for respite, not even the tender darkness behind his eyelids.

"The decades have passed. The beatings done," Mario whispered. "Pedro, look."

Pedro opened his eyes to see Mario pointing with the two fingers that held his lit cigarette.

"Down there. That's the only place you can go to finish—what did you call it? 'Taking dictation.'"

"What do you want, Mario? A recitation of the past, of colonial history? Of the greed that runs like a fuse through slaughter?"

"Calamity gives birth to goodness, Pedro. Or at least a quality of heart, something that leads to a permanent insurgency of the breast, an insurgency that never dies, even after no one is left standing. Why are you being so obtuse?" Mario paused. "Shall we see what time it is?"

"I know what time it is."

"It's time for a walk, Pedro."

"I don't want to go down there," Pedro tried to explain, gesturing vaguely toward the window. "I have work to do. I promised Sonya."

"Beautiful Sonya. You took her away."

"You're keeping me from my work."

"Your work is down there today, Pedro. It's time."

Mario's words reverberated in Pedro's head. He closed his eyes against the pressure.

"Admit it."

"I don't know what you're talking about," Pedro insisted.

CHAPTER SEVEN

★

CAMILO LEFT the history department and descended
to the main quadrangle where several hundred students
were shouting, their fists raised and moving in time to
their chant.

"¡Cayó y calló!"

"¡Cayó y calló!"

A handful of students had scrambled onto the surface
of the tank, the very one on which Fidel had ridden down
from the mountains and into the city in 1959. It had been
sitting on the quad for as long as any of the students could
remember, fossilized under a thick, protective coat of
fern-green paint. The celebratory monument to the revolution had always appeared to Camilo either threatening
or bathetic, an armored vehicle treated like a flower
pressed between the leaves of a book. The spectacle of his

peers scrambling up and latching on to the tank as if they were mounting Quijote's nag made him laugh anxiously. His classmates were clinging to every possible surface of the tank, Cuban flags and placards in hand, shouting at the top of their lungs, the rhythm of their chants clashing, raising a terrible cacophony:

"*¡Libertad! ¡Libertad! ¡Libertad!*"

"*¡Fidel cayó y Fidel calló!*"

"*¡Cuba libre! ¡Cuba libre! ¡Cuba libre!*"

From the crowd's edge, Camilo watched, hoping out of habit to see Amparo, though he knew it was useless. Amparo would never return to him. She had said so. Camilo ran his right hand over the dark stubble on his face and rubbed his eyes. Should he join them? he wondered. Instead he turned away, feeling irritated at the students, as if they had cut him adrift, separating him from his habitual routine, leaving him to float, hapless and alone, that strange emptiness he felt within himself, that thing he could fill only with drink, his only companion.

"Camilo!"

Camilo turned to see Conchita approaching, smiling wanly, her arms in long muslin sleeves that extended just beyond her fingertips.

"I can barely hear you," he said.

Camilo took her by the arm and led her away from the quad and down a nearby street. He noticed the dark, cavernous circles under Conchita's eyes.

"Friends?"

"Always, Concha."

Camilo hugged her.

"You lost more weight," he said.

Conchita crossed her arms and held them tightly against her body.

"Show me your arms, Concha."

"Just a few old scars. You're not my mother."

"Show me," Camilo insisted.

"You think they're right?" Conchita gestured back at the growing mass of students demonstrating on the quad.

"Professor Valle says they're not." Camilo shrugged. "Were you demonstrating?"

"Going to class. Now I'm trying to catch the bus," Conchita said. "Amparo isn't here."

"Did I ask?"

"You should talk to her," Conchita said. "I can say something."

"You should stop cutting yourself. It's not going to solve anything."

"I'll stop cutting when you stop avoiding Amparo."

The dark, familiar feeling that he was living a life not his own began to encroach on Camilo despite the light of the morning sun. It was a mood that usually engulfed him at night, which was why he insisted on leaving the radio on as he fell asleep, even if all he could hear was the sound of static. Of the women he had loved, only Amparo understood how unbearable that space was between conscious and unconscious worlds, how in that crossing the insignificance of his life became so palpably real to him. When Amparo was present, he felt liberated; his mood would lift, letting him feel weightless, gleeful at the smallest details, and tolerant of any ambiguity that he couldn't manage.

"I'm sorry, Camilo. I shouldn't have said that. I just wish you would say hello to her or something."

"I have to go, Concha. You could eat something. You look like a paper kite in a gale. You want a lift?"

"Camilo, you can change her mind. Talk to her."

Camilo wrapped his arms around her and said good-bye. "I'm going this way." He gestured with his chin.

Then he left her and the noisy crowd of students far behind, walking to the side street where he had left his father's Fairlane. Whenever Camilo could get gasoline on the black market, he would take the *aguacatón*, the big avocado, so dubbed by one of his little cousins in a trill of giggles for the thick green paint he had brushed over the car's rusting surface, and set off to make money shuttling tourists from point to point. He had become a taxi driver out of necessity. He needed euros. Tourists had euros and needed taxis to get around those parts of the city and the island that had been especially prepared for them. He turned the ignition, felt the shudder of the engine, and smelled the exhaust that wafted up and through the old chassis. He pulled into the stream of traffic and looked up at the morning sky and the buildings whose pastel colors seemed to be dissolving into the air.

At the age of twenty-seven, Camilo had decided to put the death of his father behind him, get married, and go back to school. One night, three years earlier, his father had gone swimming in the ocean and drowned. Afterward Camilo couldn't get it out of his head that his father had died trying to swim to the U.S. to find the woman he loved and hated—Hortensia, Camilo's mother. She had departed suddenly, during the chaotic boatlift of 1980, when the Cuban government let everyone who was clamoring to go leave, even inviting a flotilla of U.S. yachts and fishing boats to take them all away. Camilo's father never forgave her.

"The ungrateful bitch abandoned us."

Over the years, the words became his father's mantra, repeated at fever pitch and often serving as a prelude to his next drinking binge. Camilo had noticed that in the months before his death, a certain forgiveness, even sentimentality, had crept into his father's tirades, which was why Camilo became obsessed with the irony that his father had drowned trying to reach the very person he had shunned for so long. His father had died attempting to execute a gesture of hope, of possibility. Camilo was so sure of it that his own drinking binge lasted for nearly two years, until finally Amparo left him. She loved him more than he could know, she said, but she refused to live with a drunk. Amparo had lived up to her name: she had sheltered him. When he eventually pulled himself up to the edge of sobriety, the thought occurred to him that Amparo had been right all along. Even here, in this place, his mother would have wanted him to be more than a taxi driver. It was that sliver of optimism that moved him to go to school.

Camilo could scarcely remember his mother, but his fealty to her had become a source of hope, an oasis shaped and tended by a lonely and sensitive little boy, and a place to which the grown Camilo often returned for solace. He insisted to himself that whatever caused her to leave them all behind must have ached within her as big as the continent to which she had blindly departed. He wondered often about her life in the U.S. She had tried to stay in contact with them in the years immediately following her departure. His father had refused any communication, burning her letters and shunning the rare telephone call. Camilo couldn't help wondering who he would have become if she had been present in his life.

The avenue stretched endlessly before Camilo like a limitless expanse of time, yet what he felt was claustrophobia, for he knew that the sense of being free was a mirage. His mother was free. His father was free. Amparo was free, of him. He was free of nothing and no one. That's what he couldn't explain to Conchita. Each of his parents had somehow managed to escape, leaving him far behind. Amparo left him because he wouldn't stop drinking, the one thing that liberated him, at least in bouts. He could feel the walls of his life squeezing him, as palpable as the smell of gasoline, the way the Fairlane's interior seemed to wrap and bind him to itself. He found himself longing for a drink. He reached down into his shirt pocket for a cigarette. The heat of the flame made him blink. He dragged the smoke deep into his lungs and let his attention be drawn away to the sound of the engine and the pressure of his left foot on the clutch.

In addition to his many personal losses, Camilo knew privation—long queues, party-line textbooks, block spies, and rose-tinted love affairs that faded to gray within the void of every day's more pressing need for food and fuel. It was only when he was listening to Professor Valle lecture that he could come close to imagining a different life. It was less what the old man said than what he implied. For Camilo, the old professor had a rootedness and a strength that belied his age and frailty. Though he sometimes resembled a dying tree, it was a tree with an enormous taproot that had sunk itself deep into Camilo's soul, providing him with a sense of his own identity. Eventually Camilo came to understand that what appeared to him as normal was for Professor Valle an accommodation. He wondered if for the old professor the memory of that earlier life, with all its material possibilities, had faded over the course of an embargo that stretched across so many decades, or whether the memory remained with him perpetually, like the ghostly presence of an absent parent, or of a lover long gone.

Camilo flicked the cigarette ash out the window as hard as he could and thought about the differences between his father and Professor Valle. His father had never been one to think too much. Valle seemed capable of nothing else. Occasionally, as the old man was lecturing, he would pause and then, startled, glance into the faces of his students as if he had just caught a glimpse of someone he knew and was trying to avoid. This morning, Camilo had found his old professor crouching in fear between a desk and a window. What had frightened him? It occurred to Camilo that both his father and Valle were perpetually startled by life.

So much of Cuban history, Valle had told the class, is less an expression of national identity than a reaction to the impositions of a stranger's will. In that moment Valle had seemed to be singling Camilo out, referring to a failure embedded as much within Camilo as within the nation's colonial history. It was as if the old professor were pointing a finger at him as he lectured, insisting that the historical failure he was describing was also Camilo's failure, the effect of the decision Camilo had made to disconnect himself from his daily life, the decision not to act but simply to endure.

"Your mother would be here if you'd never been born," Camilo's enraged, drunken father told him.

The words, spoken early and often, had seared Camilo's consciousness. They rose in his mind now and began to settle on that tender place within him. He struck the car's horn impatiently, as if the driver in front of him was the one who had wounded him so deeply. The mother's body through which Camilo had passed, her invisible presence as an oasis of hope that sustained him, the body of a nation that had acquiesced, been imposed upon and violated; Camilo couldn't separate them. They appeared in his mind as one. He had wanted to tell Valle all this. He had wanted to explain the parts of his life that moved him to study history, yet he couldn't. He knew he should understand Valle's words, even present the old man with some sort of rebuttal, something witty, bookish, but he couldn't do that either. The edges of Valle's words slipped his conscious understanding. His mind became blank, and he felt suddenly very angry with himself, with Valle, with everything around him.

As he pulled up to a red light, Camilo noticed an old woman dressed in bundles of colorful rags trundling down the side of the road. Helping her became an instant refutation of Valle's argument, or at least a way to avoid a discomfort all the greater because he couldn't name it or touch its borders. Camilo honked the Fairlane's horn.

"Hey," he shouted at the old woman, "you need a lift?"

CHAPTER EIGHT

"¡Saturnina, Saturnina!
¿Cómo llegas a la esquina?
Caminando vas cojeando
Con tu alma pidiendo almas,
Con tus ojos de tristeza
Viendo cuanto se atraviesa."

Saturnina descended from her hovel, beckoned by the sad angel who had called to her from the entryway.

"I want to see La Milagrosa," she pleaded to the sky, her lids squeezed shut against the sun.

"¡Fidel cayó!"

"Fidel silenced!"

"¡Fidel calló!"

"Fidel fell!"

One action leads to another, the old woman thought.

The only remedy was to ask permission of everything, as if by engaging the consent of the trees and stones, the birds and insects about her, she could mitigate that terrible, invisible chain.

"I want to see La Milagrosa."

Seconds later, a swallow alighted on the branch of a nearby tree and shook its feathers, and Saturnina felt vindicated. She squatted in the dust, knees splayed under the endless folds of her skirts, palms pressed against the ground until she felt the pulse of the earth telling her to stand and walk, which she did, in the direction of the cemetery. She would confer with La Milagrosa, for Saturnina knew, after seeing and touching the blood, that the death of Fidel and his brother that morning was no illusion but an omen, a portent of something that also brought news of Tomás.

"*Oye, señora*, you need a lift?"

"I want to see La Milagrosa," Saturnina repeated, this time her eyes wide with wonder.

The legend was so well known that Saturnina assumed the cabbie knew. She watched him lean across the front seat and open the door.

Once she was seated, he twisted his head over his left shoulder and hurled the bright-green car into the hot, toxic stream of traffic, the tailpipe spilling a bluish plume of gasoline fumes into the air. Eventually, above the rattle of the engine, he called something out to her.

"*¿Qué?*"

"La Milagrosa, do you believe in her?" Camilo asked.

"Do you want to?" Saturnina answered, sensing his resistance.

"It's a nice legend."

Saturnina closed her eyes, shutting out his skepticism, and felt her body floating up toward the canopy of trees on either side of the street. The path had opened before her. It was a serious thing, this sea-monster-green taxi that had appeared suddenly, propitiously. It confirmed the seriousness of her plan and its purpose. She had to make sure she spoke to La Milagrosa, one grieving mother to another; that the desire she expressed was—and here Saturnina faltered. It would have to be large, she finally thought.

"Camilo," the old woman called out.

"*¿Qué quieres, vieja?*" The young man responded, not noticing that he had never given her his name.

"I know we haven't seen each other in a long time. I know you're scared." Saturnina hesitated. "I want you to know."

"What's that?"

"Fidel calló, Camilo."

"So I heard." Camilo shrugged, lighting another cigarette.

Saturnina cocked her left eyebrow at him and said nothing, choosing instead to watch him, to watch the heavy traffic and the city that seemed to scroll past her open window.

Camilo's *aguacatón* pulled up to the triumphal arch of the Cementerio Cristóbal Colón, the bluish plume of fuel vapors that had been trailing them for miles catching up and whipping silently over them. Saturnina did not wait for Camilo, who was sitting thoughtfully in the driver's seat. She leveraged herself out of the car, one hand pulling on either side of the door frame, and propelled herself through the cemetery's enormous arch and up its central avenue, leaving him behind. Saturnina threaded her way through the quadrants of the cemetery, through the cruciforms and measured gridwork of lesser paths, recognizing every marble angel, every tree and rail and family crypt. She passed, swaying and swirling, loading the edges of her skirts with the dry dust of midday.

"Buenos días, Condesa. Fidel cayó."

"Buenos días, Don Sampera. Fidel calló."

She greeted the aristocrats and patriarchs resting on

the other side of the baroque stone portals as if she had been their contemporary and confidante; as if the differences that even now separated the ashes of each family had never existed. She spun her way through the necropolis, as old as the New World, as every immigrant who had flooded Cuba's main harbor and left there, along with their bones, their ideas of order and beauty, of how to reconcile this life with the next. She tripped and twirled, her skirts a vortex of dust, until she came to that portion of the cemetery that had been designed and built at the end of the nineteenth century, where a life-sized marble statue of a woman holding a child in her arms stood. Around the statue were enormous heaps of flowers in various stages of decay and handwritten notes carefully impaled on the iron railing around the tomb.

Saturnina stood in the shade of the massive pine tree on the opposite side of the path and waited for Camilo to catch up to her.

"¿*Te sabes el cuento, Camilo?* The story goes she died in childbirth after a hard labor. The child died, too. Its body was placed at her feet."

Saturnina lifted her eyes toward the statue, her lips still moving, silently shaping the words only she could see hanging in midair.

"The husband was inconsolable, so he had a statue made of her. Perhaps if he could sit with her image every day, he thought. Do you sit with the dead, Camilo?"

By the look on his face, Saturnina could see that the question had caught Camilo by surprise, reminding him of something he had tried to bury deep within himself.

"If you are quiet enough, you can feel them in the air beside you. They say things."

"Like '*Fidel calló*'?"

"No, that happened this morning. He and his brother fell from a balcony near the university."

"What were they doing there?"

"Plummeting to the cobblestones of the people."

"*¿Fidel calló?*"

"*Cayó y calló.* Funny, isn't it? Both words sound the same. But they don't mean the same." Saturnina paused, glancing from Camilo's face to the sky. "Maybe they do," she decided. "Maybe they are so close, if you have one you have the other. Do you want to hear about La Milagrosa?"

Saturnina looked at him. "You're scared."

"I'm hot," Camilo insisted.

He tugged at his thin, short-sleeved shirt, damp with perspiration, stuck to his back and chest.

"Your stomach is churning with fear." Saturnina laughed. "You're afraid of a statue—or a promise?"

"I'm not afraid of anything."

"I'm not an old woman," Saturnina said, winking at Camilo.

"What about La Milagrosa?"

"Her husband was crushed by grief. So he had a beautiful marble statue of her made. That way he could look at her every day. When the workers unearthed the coffin to install the statue, he couldn't resist. He ordered the coffin opened, and they discovered the baby they had put to rest at her feet was now in her arms. It looked as if it was nursing at her breast. For the first time since her death, a strange peace came over him. He had a new statue made of her holding the infant. *Por alguna razón, Camilo.* He knew it was a miracle. Something greater than anything we can see or understand moved that child into her arms. It helped her husband find peace."

The old woman rasped her words, all the while staring at Camilo until she could see the calamities of his life flickering across his forehead.

"The story got around. Then everyone started coming here to pray for miracles. They would ask for things." She smiled, shaking the bag of tesserae at her side.

"Then some people started to say you must never turn your back on La Milagrosa. It would be like turning your back on hope. Now they plead and walk backward, bowing low, but never turning away from her."

Saturnina grasped Camilo's forearm as if it were a thick rope and let herself down into a squat. She began to intone her prayer, eyes pressed tight, mouth moving in silent rhythm to the loose rosary of tesserae clicking in her hand. She rocked forward and back on her haunches in the dust, a wrinkled child lulling itself to sleep, an old dragon breathing fire through its nostrils.

"*Fidel cayó y Fidel calló.* He silenced and he fell."

Saturnina felt Camilo reaching down, placing his hands on her shoulders, as if he were about to shake her the way any taxi driver might shake a slumbering passenger, but Saturnina reached up and grasped his forearms, letting him pull her up instead.

"*Sí, Camilo.* You haven't heard a word I've said, have you? *Fidel cayó y Fidel calló.* Don't turn your back. Don't walk away again, Camilo. Tomás needs you. You need him."

Saturnina could see that her words, spoken with the softness of dandelion plush in a midsummer breeze, angered Camilo, who could muster no other response to his rising anxiety. Standing, Saturnina raised her arms gently along her sides and called out to her belovéd Milagrosa, slowly walking backward. A minute or two later, Camilo began to walk backward, trailing after the old woman.

CHAPTER NINE

★

CAMILO DECIDED TO ACT as if he believed. He followed Saturnina, walking backward with her, always facing the statue of La Milagrosa until it was out of sight. Then they both faced forward, and he continued to follow a few paces behind her as she wandered through the cemetery, pausing at certain tombs. He couldn't help noticing that this visit wasn't personal. She didn't seem to have a loved one buried here; the tombs where she paid her respects were too ancient.

"What are you doing?"

Saturnina turned to Camilo, her eyes wide, surprised by the question.

"I have to tell everyone."

"About La Milagrosa?"

"Fidel calló, Camilo."

"Can they hear you?" Camilo pointed at the tombs nearby.

Saturnina couldn't control the tone of exasperation in her voice.

"Unbelief will destroy you, Camilo."

Camilo watched as the old woman rocked back and forth on her haunches under the shade of the pine trees where they had paused to rest from the heat.

"Do you have any family? Someone who looks after you?"

"Yes, he'll be here soon."

"Who?"

"Tomás. What a strange question, Camilo."

Saturnina began to recite the facts of Tomás's death as if she were repeating the litany of a mass, the faraway expression in her eyes suggesting how time had stopped for her one day in 1956.

"I had just finished the dishes. Vania, my daughter-in-law, was upstairs visiting a neighbor. Someone knocked. When I opened the door, it was Armando."

"I thought you said his name was Tomás?"

"Armando was Tomás's classmate. The boys used to tease him. He always had such a tragic look on his face. There he was telling me something happened to Tomás.

That's what he said. 'Something happened.' Then he looked down at the floor as if he had dropped his keys and wanted very much to find them again. I remember thinking no one hesitates to say something good happened. Vania came down the stairs and saw him. It wasn't until she started to cry that I knew. Armando told me everything later. Then I began to see."

Camilo reached out gently and placed the palm of his hand on her arm, drawing her into the present again.

"What was he like?"

"Armando?"

"Your son."

"He's your son, too, Camilo. He had a beautiful smile. Perfect, white teeth. Everyone said so. Did you forget him already?"

"I never knew him."

"Are you sure?"

"We've just met."

"You're Camilo. Tomás's father."

"I'm Camilo Santos. I never knew your son."

Saturnina looked at him, puzzled, uncertain why someone she had known so intimately would insist on being someone else.

"*Santos*? Was that your path, Camilo? From sinner to saint?" Saturnina smiled broadly, revealing the gaps in her teeth. "Well, why not? Shame you never stuck around long enough to see. That child of ours grew straight and strong. Like a royal palm. I'm glad I knew him—as a young man, a married man. That's something, isn't it? I was allowed to see something of who he was. You didn't have that, did you?"

"You're confusing me with another Camilo."

"There is only one Camilo. I can keep your secret if you want me to." She winked impishly at him.

"What did Armando tell you?"

"That Tomás died for what he believed."

"They weren't just classmates?"

"They were friends."

"Your son was a Fidelista?"

"Our son hated what Batista was doing."

"He opposed Batista?"

"He thought Cuba was for Cubans, not Yankees. Which party was that?"

Camilo looked at her. The old woman's entire face seemed to quiver with the quiet frankness of her question.

"What did Armando say?"

"When?"

"About Tomás's death."

"Armando was standing next to him. Someone had just told a joke. They were all laughing. He remembered hearing someone call out Tomás's name. He turned around when Tomás did."

"What did he see?"

"A man dressed in black."

"Another classmate?"

"Armando said it was CIA. All of it."

Saturnina began to rock on her haunches like a distracted child.

"It had something to do with Tomás's detention. Just before Tomás died. You know, when I first saw Armando at the door that day, I thought to myself, 'Oh, Tomás has been detained again. How will we get him out this time? Who will we have to bribe? Where will we find the money this time?' It was worse than that, wasn't it?"

Saturnina began to sob, her eyes shut tight, her fists squeezing the folds of fabric in her lap.

"It's my fault. I didn't protect him. The night before, Camilo, I was so happy. Vania was pregnant. We were sitting around the table after dinner. I went to bed dreaming of my first grandchild. I had no premonition half my heart would be gone the next day. When Tomás left for school in the morning, he was whistling. '*No, Mamá,* I'll have your lovely coffee later.' He gave me a kiss and bolted out the door. I never saw him alive again."

"What happened to Armando?"

"He thought it was his fault."

"Was it?"

"No. They all loved Tomás. The protests they organized. The things they did. They looked to him to tell them. Our son knew how to lead, Camilo. How to stay quiet, to listen. Tomás taught me how to listen."

She was smiling through her tears now, looking at Camilo to gauge his understanding. To Camilo, she sounded child-like. The lack of guile in her words confused him. That ancient face with its eyes behind their cataract scrim looking at him like some Madonna that had appeared, not in luminous blue robes hovering in the sky above him, her face glowing beatifically, but in tatters, with a patina of filth over her, pushing through the swollen folds of dark earth and now sitting before him.

"Tomás would have hated this."

The old woman gestured with her head as if to indicate

her son's opposition to the ambient air. Camilo understood what she meant: Tomás, opposed to the brutality of Batista, would have been opposed as well to what the revolution had become.

"Words are only ever half true, Camilo."

She started to rock back and forth on her haunches as if she were lulling herself to sleep. Camilo could sense that she had traveled elsewhere again in her mind.

"I know who killed him." The tears rolled down Saturnina's face. She worked to push the corners of her mouth into a smile as if it were her only barricade against a tidal wave of sorrow.

"The first time Batista's men detained him, he returned home badly beaten. The second time, they beat him again. The third time, they didn't touch him. They released him. They waited. Then they tracked him down like an animal and killed him. I'm his mother. I should have known. The morning he left, I had no premonition. I should have warned him, but I didn't. I didn't protect him. I didn't even say good-bye properly."

She looked at Camilo directly, her eyes wide with anxiety.

"Remember what I told you about La Milagrosa?" she asked. "Her husband found peace."

Camilo tried to imagine how she must have struggled to rationalize the brutality, the terrible magnitude of her loss.

"Many times grace is fierce, Camilo." She reached across and clasped his forearm with both of her arthritic hands. "Like the day you left me."

"Tell me about the assassin—"

"That child of God—"

"He killed your son."

Saturnina's attention was drawn away by something in the distance, or maybe she was consciously ignoring Camilo. Whatever the reason, she let Camilo's words hang in the air.

"I don't know that I could forgive that much," Camilo confessed, slouching forward.

"I forgave you for leaving me so far behind. I never cursed you for it. I never did. Never."

She looked at him, a shy smile forming.

Camilo took another cigarette and lit it, inhaled deeply, and watched Saturnina's face closely, as if it were a map that would lead him to some secret place within himself. He tried to release his anxiety along with the smoke he blew out through his mouth, but the anxiety remained, leaving him with a terrible thirst to forget how poorly he fit inside his own skin.

They had reached the *aguacatón*. Once inside, Camilo switched on the ignition and pulled away from the curb and into the street.

"That's Pablo's problem, too." Saturnina smiled at Camilo through the broken panes of her teeth, her face still wet with tears. She felt calm, having dispensed to the dead the startling news of the day.

"You want another drink, don't you, Camilo? You always did whenever something upset you."

"Who's Pablo?" Camilo asked, studiously refusing to remind her that she was mistaking him for someone else.

"Vania picked a good man the first time. The second time a worm picked her."

"A real worm?"

"He did live in the United States for a while. What I mean is he'd sell his own mother. I never thought of it before, but you're like Pablo."

"I never knew my mother. She left when I was still very young."

"You always drank to forget. You never hit me."

"You're confusing me with someone else, Saturnina."

"You drink to forget."

Saturnina's words settled on Camilo, attaching themselves sharply to his skin. He couldn't swat them off without revealing the wounds that had disfigured him, the losses and the terrible sense of abandonment he felt. Mother, father, lover—all Camilo could see any longer was the cruelty of their absence. The response he had taught himself over the course of his life was a willful cutting away of whatever he chose not to acknowledge.

"You understand," she insisted, turning away, looking at him almost coyly. "We must forgive all the tyrants."

"Even the ones who killed Tomás?"

"It's all part of something larger that never ends. He will return, Camilo."

"What happened to Tomás's friends?"

"They tried to overthrow Batista. They were killed or died in jail. But not Armando. 'If only I had stepped in, taken the gun away,' he kept saying. 'I could have taken the gun away.' Poor Armandito. He told me afterward that he couldn't bear to be in a crowd. He would pull back and wait if he heard someone calling out his name."

"What about Vania?"

"Vania was lost after Tomás's death. I would find her sitting on the couch near the balcony doors, as still as a statue, gazing out at nothing, just waiting. I think she thought if she didn't move, time would stand still. And if she could make time stand still, then maybe she could make it wind back, too. Maybe she could change what happened. Sitting in the house with her was like sitting through a dead calm on the ocean. The deep currents underneath us. Above the surface, nothing. She grieved that way for a long time. Even when she did start doing the things she normally did, she looked like she was sleeping with her eyes open."

"The worm broke the spell?"

"*Sí, un gusano* gnawed its way through the woodwork. Strange how he crawled up from nowhere. He knew all the right things to say to her, too. Such a romantic fellow—at least before he started to beat her."

"Maybe you were jealous—for your son's sake."

"Whenever I looked into his eyes, I could hear him, clickety click, clickety click, that little head of his spinning like a cheap clock. He was always calculating something no one else could see."

"Vania had money?"

"Vania was his assignment."

Camilo glanced at the old woman.

"Pablo married her in order to gather information on dissident groups."

"She was a dissident?"

"No, but he thought she was because she had married Tomás. Whoever he was working for thought so, too.

After the revolution, he stayed with her for his own safety. He never believed she would denounce her own husband. Lazy bastard. Lived on whatever Vania could provide, especially during the leanest years of the embargo."

"Poor Vania."

"I'll say. Sleeping with one of Batista's spies, a good-for-nothing husband who never worked a day in his life and beat her, too. At first he'd get payments from an American who would show up at the door every month. 'He's an old family friend,' he told us, 'from when I lived in the States,' but he wouldn't let anyone else answer the door. He threatened to lock us in one of the bedrooms if we dared. The two of them would hide in the dining room and talk for hours. This went on from the time he married Vania. That was in '58. It lasted about three years. Right after the visit there would be plenty of money to spend."

"What did Vania do?"

"She married Pablo because she was lonely. She made a terrible mistake. She didn't understand until later. Then it was too late. Their lives were all tangled up together. She couldn't bear any more loss. Marrying him made her even lonelier. She came to believe that she deserved the beatings, deserved the way he barked and spat at her."

Saturnina dug into the pouch at her side and finally spilled its contents into her lap. From among the tesserae, she excavated a small blue plastic box, the sort a child might fill with marbles and string and pieces of found treasure. Inside, wrapped in aluminum foil dull with creases, was a photograph.

Camilo stopped the *aguacatón* at an intersection unusually jammed with traffic and looked at the photograph Saturnina had handed him. He saw a younger Saturnina standing before an enormous red hibiscus bush—upright, perched like a ballerina about to make some delicate leap in the air. Her skin looked lighter. Her hair pulled back tightly and her smile intact, she looked barely older than her son, who stood between her and a young woman with a shy smile, more petite than Saturnina. Tomás held both women close to him, his face handsome and his smile brilliant, engaging. He had crouched slightly in order to tuck his mother and his wife within his open embrace, which seemed broad enough to include whoever was behind the camera and gave Tomás the appearance of an enormous bird, body arched, gazing up now toward Camilo. The photograph had been taken almost two years before Tomás's death, according to the date carefully handwritten on the back.

"My mother was there the day he was born. I wish you had been there to see your son, Camilo." Saturnina cackled with glee. "That was before you became a *santos*."

It occurred to Camilo that Saturnina was still a girl when she gave birth to her son, after someone, another Camilo, had abandoned her.

CHAPTER TEN

★

PEDRO VALLE DESCENDED from his office, walking as fast as he could away from the university and the expanding number of milling, chanting students. He went down toward Lealtad, toward the seawall, leaving his office perch, barely remembering to close and lock his door behind him. He had stuffed the yellowing pages of his manuscript into his worn leather briefcase, avoided the secretary, and skirted along the perimeter of the quadrangle, running from whatever lay beneath the terrible agitation he felt and hoping Mario would appreciate that he had found the courage to do as he had asked.

Pedro walked east down Avenida San Miguel and crossed the broad Calzada de Infanta with barely a glance to either side. He pushed on like a dreamer treading the redundant landscape of his subconscious, propelled forward by anxiety and an inchoate need to resolve the turmoil he felt. He crossed Avenida Padre Varela and then turned on Lealtad and began to walk toward the Caleta de San Lázaro, striving toward the curving body of water named after the saint who was called back to life, watching the seawall and the ocean grow larger with each step. Finally, rounding Lealtad, he saw ocean and curving stone balcony hinged together in space like some impossible butterfly with enormous wings of water and earth. Softly to round the corner of Lealtad was to drop into the infinite clarity of the Caribbean. To press his hand against the masonry was to feel himself outside the flow of time, the weight of his sorrows lifted. In that moment he was as elemental as the stone, as the sprays of saltwater leaping high above the seawall. In that stillness lay everything Pedro Valle loved, and in the rhythm of that immutable embrace he could find respite.

Across the avenue was the seawall, El Malecón. Once he reached it, Pedro turned to look back at the city. The long rows of houses seemed to be imploding; invisible cascades of dust falling, their accumulated weight pressing forward like a crowd of people pushing against an obstacle. Houses once painted the color of summer skies, of yellow butterflies, of coral rose petals had faded now, the gray pall of exposed plaster encroaching upward by slow inches. The plate tectonics of mortar and stone pressing, sliding against one another: downward alignment—a finding of the earth, the pull of the magnetic core, the press of gravity. It was not simply a tableau of decay but of resistance, of columns chipped, yet still bearing the weight of carved impediments, of interiors hollowed out by time and yet somehow still inhabited by people.

Pedro heard something like the roar of voices in a crowded restaurant, escalating as each person attempts to be heard over the din. It wasn't just a sound; it was a change in pressure against his eardrums, like a shift in barometric pressure before a storm. In the interval between the waves striking the seawall, drops of saltwater fanning upward into the air, the cellophane effervescence of the foam crumpling against sand and stone, a wave drew itself back and left, at the bottom of that gargantuan, magnetic inhalation, a pause.

Looking out across the avenue and toward the city, Pedro could see people peering from the crumbling balconies and worn window frames of the low three- and four-story buildings that lined San Nicolás. He could see people gathering on rooftops; emerging cautiously from doorways; standing on San Nicolás and facing the center of the

city, gingerly drawn down along its worn cobblestone trajectory. Some of the waiters at the tented restaurants along
the seawall had stopped their preparations and let their
attention be drawn toward the city, as if it represented
some magical center. The tables behind them were empty,
not a single tourist had descended from the grassy rise of
the Hotel Nacional for an early lunch; not a gaggle anywhere of bright pink Europeans walking thickly, feet
splayed, belly first, in quivering straw hats and rubber flip-
flops. Pedro pushed away from the emptiness like a man
seated at table, opening a breach between himself and its
surface, a stillness and absence of feeling that he believed
would keep him separate and safe.

Pedro heard the roar of an engine and turned to see
the cars traveling on the broad boulevard swerving to
avoid a rusty black 1953 Citroën that was careening madly
across the traffic lanes. The closer the Citroën got, the
more it seemed to Pedro like a clown car stuffed with
passengers, festooned with dozens of small Cuban flags
that flapped violently in the wind. Pedro could see the
balding heads and sagging jowls of the middle-aged passengers. He could hear a familiar *bolero* blasting from the
car's speakers.

The Citroën circled around and around; with each

turn the hilarity of the men escalated. Two men sat on the open windows of the car doors, holding on for dear life, while the men inside howled with laughter at their impromptu lyrics.

"Siempre que te pregunto
Sí Fidel calló y como,
Tu siempre me respondes
Quizás, quizás, quizás."

Pedro was mesmerized by the spinning Citroën, as were the drivers of the oncoming cars who stopped to witness the men's antics. He expected the other drivers to be angry. Instead some of them got out of their cars to get a better look, and others sat honking their approval, keeping time to the music. The driver of the Citroën stuck his bald head out the window again like a dog never allowed a single pleasure.

"Vamos," he shouted, gesturing to the other drivers before launching into another lyric.

"Hoy estas pensando
No tengo comida.
Ya no sufras mas que
Calló, calló, calló."

Everyone shouted the last line in unison. The Citroën

made one last dizzying spin and blasted away, the other drivers speeding after it.

A wave of anxiety rolled through Pedro, lifting, pushing him into the past, his mind confused, the sound of the Citroën's gunning engine, the *bolero* blaring from the car's speakers, the drivers honking—all of these reverberating in his ears until he couldn't separate past from present.

"It's time to do something, Pedro. Come with me."

"To serve as witness? Go headlong into that fray, Mario?"

"Let's go, Pedro."

The memory caused Pedro to sink into the distress rising up from his belly. He could hear the cellophane sound of the waves as they gathered, preparing to strike the seawall, the sound of the waves transforming itself into the din of the café near the university that last time he saw Mario, patrons' voices vaulting one over the other, forks and knives clattering against plates, chairs scudding against linoleum, the radio blaring. Mario had always been drawn to the center of whatever was happening in a way that frightened Pedro. The slightest whiff of injustice and there Mario would be; no matter how hopeless, how dire, he would step into every fray.

"Don't do this, Mario. Don't risk your life."

"Come with me. I mimeographed the notice."

"Put that away. Someone will see it. We have to deny everything we've seen or said, Mario."

"No, Pedro. We have to claim all of it. We have to say what we want."

Pedro shook his head, his mind blank with fear.

"They'll kill us. The goons on the right. The goons on the left. It won't matter."

The words hung in the air between them, the blunt force of which Mario tried to diminish, closing his eyes, turning his head in profile as if the words were fists glancing off the line of his jaw. Pedro could see the anger tacit in Mario's gesture.

"Think this through, Mario. It's one thing to be a popular teacher—"

"I don't want to sit and think. Not now."

"They will kill you."

"Then you'll finish—"

"Finish what? You can't stake your life—"

"Give your testimony. Write it down. Tell the story of whatever this is that's happening around us. Only time will tell."

Mario's words made Pedro quiver like a tuning fork.

Just past Mario's right shoulder, Pedro could see the café owner's youngest daughter, a broad red ribbon in her hair, sitting at the cash register by the door, pushing back her cuticles with the eraser tip of a pencil, then reaching for the radio and turning up the volume.

"Siempre que te pregunto
Que donde, cuando y como,
Tu siempre me respondes
Quizás, quizás, quizás."

The lovelorn voice of the singer, the lines of the old *bolero*; Pedro remembered how they seemed to mock the two of them, Mario and he, leaning over the Formica tabletop as they argued back and forth.

"They will kill you, Mario."

"Quizás, quizás, quizás."

"Then you'll finish the manifesto for me."

"Quizás, quizás, quizás."

That day so many years ago, after Mario left the café, Pedro waited what he thought would seem a reasonable amount of time, drained his cup, and asked for the check. Had anyone overheard them? Had anyone understood? At the cash register, the owner's youngest daughter was humming under her breath as she made change.

"Professor, haven't you forgotten something?" The

girl was smiling at him, pointing with a roughly manicured finger at the new leather briefcase Sonya and Mario had given him. He had left it by his chair.

"My *papi*'s absentminded, too." She grinned, clamping down on the piece of gum between her teeth.

"I'm not used to carrying one. I keep forgetting," Pedro stammered, smiling sheepishly at the girl behind the cash register.

An enormous wave crashed against the seawall. Pedro turned to face the sea. He gripped the wall's broad ledge and forced himself to lean forward toward the very thing he feared most, the way he remembered leaning over the café table; remembered the inverted aluminum cone of the light fixture swaying gently over Mario's head and his as the door near the cash register opened and closed and people streamed in and out. He and Mario had argued fiercely, had leaned their bodies in toward one another, their whispers turning into sibilant hisses, drawing curious stares. No, Pedro had repeated; but Mario had insisted and passed to him across the café table what he had written on that white sheet of paper, now neatly folded in two. He remembered Mario's exasperation, his long tapered fingers as they pushed the folded sheet past the dull metal coffee pot, the covered bowl encrusted with damp sugar, the teaspoons with their residue of coffee, the demitasse clattering, its lip bleeding coffee into the saucer, and the way one corner of the sheet of paper wicked the dark liquid. Mario had written a call to join across political lines and demand democratic reforms, a halt to U.S. intervention, and then copied it hundreds of times over on the mimeograph machine in the art department office long after the staff had left for the day.

The memory caused something to rise in Pedro's throat and almost lift him off his feet. To find the ground again, he closed his eyes. He could see the sheet his interrogators had dropped on the table before him in the dimly lit cell. The neatly folded sheet with the coffee stain had been smudged by something more viscous, something that repelled and attracted him, as if Mario was already reaching back to him across the chasm between life and death. The sheet that bore witness to that moment across the table, the soft light of the aluminum cone holding Mario and Pedro together in a trine of light and flesh and friendship. That sheet and the two friends leaning over the tabletop, over coffee and spilled sugar and soiled teaspoons; that had been the moment of Mario's death, not later, when he was picked up off the street and disappeared. When Mario was made to disappear, Pedro

CHAPTER ELEVEN

★

CAMILO STOPPED the *aguacatón* at an intersection jammed with traffic.

"*Oye*," Saturnina called out from the passenger-side window. "*¿Que hora es?*"

The farmer who was frantically loading melons back into his large wooden cart stopped to look at the wristwatch he had tied with string to his belt loop. He called back to her over his shoulder:

"*La una y pico.*"

"This is my stop," Saturnina told Camilo, and he pulled over to the curb.

"Is this where you live, Saturnina?"

Camilo pointed to the building adjacent to the rubble-strewn lot where the farmer had parked his cart.

"No, over there."

She had already opened the door of the *aguacatón*, slid off the seat, and begun making her way among the cars idling on the congested street. She gestured toward a façade opposite to where she stood that seemed to be propped up by the buildings that flanked it. The entrance arch was intact and covered in brilliant white tiles with deep blue arabesques.

"It's already past one o'clock. I'll see you later, Camilo." This last she called out over her shoulder as she waved the backs of her raised arms at him.

Camilo sat in the bumper-to-bumper traffic absorbing the emptiness her departure evoked in him. He lit another cigarette and inhaled deeply, feeling strangely irritated at how, for the second time that day, someone had set him adrift. He could feel the black fog lurking on the perimeter, waiting to engulf him; that terrible sense of loss he could only tamp down with drink. He glanced into the rearview mirror, but he couldn't see the face reflected there, only his eyes bleary with disappointment. He could feel within himself the desire for a gesture that would define him, that would open him to the gift of accepting his losses. Camilo snorted at the irony of whatever Valle and Saturnina had unearthed in him. He tried to shake off the anger he suddenly felt toward them both, toward Amparo, toward everyone who had abandoned him.

He pulled away from the curb, launching the *aguacatón* into traffic. Then he reached into his shirt pocket for another cigarette and noticed it was his last one. His friend Eliel, who was always trading on the black market, would have some. His house was out in Fontanal, though, one of the city's suburbs, and Camilo needed cigarettes now. He remembered a little bar nearby that sometimes sold them and on impulse found a spot to park the *aguacatón*.

The bar was only the verandah of an old wooden house that sat on the corner of a side street. On one end was a long counter where a hungry-looking middle-aged man stood serving drinks. In front of the counter were half-a-dozen mismatched stools. Plastic tables and lawn chairs were scattered randomly from one end of the verandah to the other. Camilo entered and asked for a pack of cigarettes. The handful of men drinking beer nearby fell silent. The bartender asked Camilo if he wanted a beer. Camilo nodded and without hesitation held up three fingers.

He found a spot at the far end of the verandah and sat hunched over the table, quickly pouring each can of Chispa de tren down his throat, hoping the cold liquid would assuage the ache he had felt in his belly all morning. He observed the *framboyan* trees in the sweltering heat, their flat dark-green fronds like fans suspended in midair, not a gust of ocean breeze stirring the soft tear-shaped petals of each frond. The coldness of the beer numbed him and gave him an interval of peace, however fleeting. Camilo opened the pack of cigarettes, took a cigarette out and quickly lit it, dragging as deeply as he could before blowing the smoke out through his nose. He realized he was sitting on the edge of the lawn chair and let himself slide all the way back.

"*¿Otra cervesa?*"

Camilo looked up at the bartender standing before him collecting the empty cans and indicated with a gesture that he wanted a shot of rum instead. The bartender obliged, sizing Camilo up as the young man was reaching into his pocket for money.

"Hear the rumors about Fidel and his brother?"

Shocked that the old woman's words were being repeated by the bartender, Camilo said nothing. In response to Camilo's silence, the bartender started to pull away, shrugging his shoulders as if to confirm the patent absurdity of the rumor.

"It's true," Camilo finally stammered. "I picked someone up in my cab who saw the whole thing."

The bartender looked at him for a moment and then
walked back to the bar. Camilo became aware of the conversations around him. The men were arguing in low
voices, only their gestures revealing their agitation.

Were Saturnina's words true, or did Camilo simply
want to believe her? He thought about the morning's
events: the cancellation of old Valle's class, the gathering
of the students in the quadrangle, the old woman's story
about how Fidel had fallen to the level of the people once
again. The same old woman who believed in La Milagrosa. What would Amparo think? Camilo flicked the
cigarette butt as hard as he could at the trunk of a *framboyan* tree and raised two fingers to the bartender.

The bartender walked over, but this time, it was
Camilo who spoke first.

"Tell them." Camilo nodded toward the men.
"It's true."

The bartender looked at him, squinting.

"I picked someone up in my taxi this morning. She
witnessed the whole thing."

"You're drunk."

"I've never been more sober. Tell them," Camilo repeated.

Camilo paid the bartender, threw back both shots, and tucked the cigarette pack into the front pocket of his shirt. He stood up slowly and tried to find his feet. The bartender had disappeared into the group of men. Camilo couldn't bear facing them, repeating for them the old woman's testimony. The certainty he had expressed to the bartender had disappeared as quickly as the shots and the few dollars he had intended to save. Camilo stood there, between table and chair, his mind swaying like his body, searching for equilibrium. There were now at least two dozen men scattered across the broken sidewalk, not including those who had spilled out from the bar. Camilo heard the clear bass voice of someone at the center of the crowd and saw the bartender pointing directly at him. Everyone's eyes seemed to follow the bartender's pointing finger.

"It's true," Camilo stammered again. He reached for the verandah's railing and hoisted his legs over the top, dropping to the ground below, then scurried away as fast as he could to find the *aguacatón*, his head aching, his heart pounding in fear.

Instead of being dissuaded by Camilo's retreat, though, the crowd of men read into his haste a justification and model for their own response. Clearly, time was of the essence. They had to act now. Whatever life they had known up to this point had been changed in an instant. They had only to recognize and embrace it. A new life. A shedding of the old. Each one of them was as terrified as the next and yet utterly incapable of speaking his fears or hesitating. To hesitate now would be a sort of death-in-life, one of them argued. That was exactly what they had endured thus far, another man insisted. They must vault the barricade they had built with their fear. They must do just as the younger man had shown them.

"Where's he going?" one of the men asked.

"He must be heading for La Plaza de la Revolucíon."

"That's where everyone's heading," the bartender yelled. "Let's go," he insisted, waving in the air the baseball bat he kept behind the bar.

The men started running after Camilo and toward the plaza, weaving their way through the streets, sure of nothing but a sense of possibility. As they ran, they were joined along the way by others who saw in them a call to action, a coherent response to the morning's news.

Camilo could hear the shouts of the men behind him as they began to mobilize. What he had just set in motion frightened him. His head throbbing, the words he had spoken seemed to belong to someone else. He couldn't recall why he had trusted the old woman or concluded she spoke truthfully. He reached the *aguacatón* and got in, slamming the heavy door behind him. He felt the panic of having told an impossible lie, one that might get him arrested or killed. He sat clenching the steering wheel, trying to think through what he had done, wanting to avoid the stupidity of the words he had uttered, the shame of having done something so ruinous to himself.

Camilo turned the ignition, heard the boom and roar of the engine, smelled the gasoline fumes that seeped into the cab. Nauseated, he rolled down the window, shifted into reverse, hooked his left arm over the window frame, and started to pull into the street, but he couldn't. Every lane was inundated with cars. People were streaming over the sidewalks, flowing like rivulets among the idling vehicles. A crowd was blocking the intersection ahead. Camilo became aware of people shouting, chanting something he couldn't quite make out over the blaring horns, the sound of drumming, of metal and wood being struck together.

"¡*Fidel calló! Fidel calló!*"

Camilo turned off the engine and got out of the *agua-catón*. He stepped on the front fender and climbed up on the car's hood. He was startled by what was happening around him. For as far as he could see, *Habaneros* had poured themselves into the streets. Stranger still, he felt he was part of this enormous mass.

"*¡Fidel calló!*" they shouted.

"*¡Fidel calló!*" Camilo shouted back.

As he stood on the hood of the car, the words burst out of him as if he had been holding his breath for a very long time. The percussive beat of those stamping feet, of people knocking together pots and ladles, hammers and tire irons, whatever they had in hand, as if the act of making noise rendered them visible for the very first time in their lives, Camilo could hear them—not the way he had heard the students earlier that day while he was standing on the perimeter of the main quad, hoping he would see Amparo, but as if the sounds they were making emanated from him, transforming him into the source and center of the crowd.

"*¡Fidel calló!*" they shouted.

"*¡Fidel calló!*" he bellowed from the hood of the *agua-catón*. His body pulsed with a newfound energy.

The crowd around him roared and swayed, in turn echoing his words like congregants at a mass.

"*¡Fidel calló!*"

Their eyes were on Camilo. For an instant, an expectant silence fell over the crowd as if they were all taking an enormous, synchronized breath. Within Camilo that instant stretched and deepened into an eternity, and he leapt into the emptiness without any expectation, only the sense that there was no other alternative for him, for his life. Whether they clapped or jeered, raised him on their shoulders or trampled him underfoot—nothing was comprehensible to him in that moment but the wide sense of movement, of action propelled by the intersection of instinct and chance.

The moment had unmoored Camilo. He emerged that day from the ground he shared with the people around him; and in that moment, as he stood above them on the hood of his father's Fairlane, he was recognizable to them. What he called out to the crowd was their history—a story, an idea of themselves he had learned listening to Professor Valle, a story that felt like a river that rushed through him, by turns deep then shallow, tranquil then churning rapidly downward in search of its ocean source. It was the terrible river he had first known as a boy, after the exile of his mother, and then later, after the loss of his father, after Amparo left him. It was the terrible river whose navigation old Valle had taught him, the way a father teaches his son.

Looking out above the roaring crowd, Camilo could see how the day's news had flowed across the city's streets, forming eddies of neighbors who clustered together and then dispersed, only to hear the same news again, with some variation, that variation eroding doubt, reformulating itself as certainty, rising like some inexorable tide, hope vaulting over time-bound anxieties. Some of the groups dispersed again. Other groups headed into the city, toward La Plaza de la Revolución, where Che Guevara's abstracted image hung. Standing atop the *aguacatón*'s hood, Camilo could see how the calm assertiveness with which he had told his compatriots they were free had opened the invisible sluice gates, giving this enormous human mass its direction and thrust. They surged past him, tens of thousands of men and women, all of them making a tremendous noise, leaving him rocking in their wake, surprisingly sober and calm and content with whoever it was he had suddenly become.

CHAPTER TWELVE

A GUST OF WIND came over the seawall, spinning the sand into small twisters, mixing the smell of seaweed and brine with the smell of gasoline and fried food. The sand stung Pedro's face and neck. He started laughing gently, the tears of his grief welling up as he recalled the smell wafting up through the floor vents of the campus building where he had sat one placid winter afternoon listening to an American, a visiting fellow, lecturing. He remembered the comic gentility with which they all ignored the musty smell of the benefactress who lay moldering next to her family, entombed in marble in the basement of the building where the history faculty and their guests sat listening politely.

That day, Pedro had sat next to a man, just younger than he, impeccably dressed, who seemed to absorb through his eyes every word spoken by the American about the island's early colonial history. The American spoke in heavily accented Spanish, and after a quarter of an hour, Pedro grew tired of listening, of silently correcting him. The American's sentences had become a conveyor belt moving at some unreasonable speed, and Pedro found himself growing frustrated, then bored, shifting all too often in his chair.

The man sitting next to Pedro hung on every word, keeping track of every tangent of the American's argument. Later, at lunch, it was that same man who countered, lobbing one objection after another at the poor fellow who (and this Mario would later say, laughing uncontrollably) had traveled all the way there to impress Caliban's heirs with his knowledge of their history.

Pedro felt another blast of wind and sand. He glanced away from the sea and saw Mario standing beside him.

"That was the first time I met you."

"I remember. It shouldn't make you cry, Pedro."

"How could I have known that the stranger sitting next to me, listening so intently, would mean to me the difference between living and dying? That you would keep me alive when all I wanted was to die?"

"You survived. Why doesn't that matter to you?"

"The debt's too large," Pedro said. "Do you remember what you said to the American fellow after the lecture? 'At the heart of every historical epoch is that same brutality which becomes easier and easier to rationalize.'"

Mario's words had been measured, each one placed like a tangible object for them to consider. A deafening silence fell over the scholars seated at the table. Pedro remembered looking a little too studiously at the play of sunlight in his water glass, hearing the sound of a coffee spoon tapping brightly, methodically against the china, seeing out of the corner of his eye someone at a far table in the dining room turning and gesturing for the waiter. Mario remained oblivious to anyone's discomfort, smiling at everything before him like some inscrutable Buddha. When the American fellow insisted that there were now, as never before, new ways of saving lives, Mario cut him off midsentence, his voice a perfectly balanced knife.

"You have better, more barbaric ways of killing. You can even kill anonymously from great distances now. But your reason for killing remains the same—coveting what isn't yours. The blunders of every empire are always a matter of wanting more. You should look instead at the fear that drives you."

Pedro remembered watching the two men carefully.

The impeccably dressed Mario was gazing steadily, serenely at the American, and Pedro could feel within himself an oceanic roil of admiration and repulsion. There Mario sat, and what struck Pedro most was his self-containment, a confidence that was as charming as it was unassailable, its source seemingly fathomless, inextinguishable. That extraordinary equilibrium that Pedro would have so many opportunities to observe and which came off sometimes as arrogance; that unquantifiable sense Mario demonstrated that whatever he thought or did was never anything but correct because he had thought about it freely and deeply and come to some determination, one way or the other. There was, too, the fact that Mario had a charisma that Pedro never would: the readiness of the smile that Mario could flash and shutter so impetuously, so intuitively, that drew its light upward and held it deeply in his eyes. No one, man or woman, could resist Mario's charm, which lay so firmly nestled in what could only be termed his genuineness.

"I didn't side with you that day. I defended the indefensible. I didn't want the American to think I was just another angry native," Pedro said. "'People lie,' that's what you said to the American. You asked him, 'What keeps you from thinking that ideological lies can't also become cultural?'"

"The first lie, that's the one we tell ourselves when we look but don't want to see. As for the question, the point wasn't that you didn't side with me. The point was that you, and everyone else at the table, avoided the question."

Someone, Pedro couldn't remember who, had tentatively sided with Mario, bringing up the Treaty of Aix-la-Chapelle that Spain, France, and Britain had all signed in 1748. The Europeans pointedly excluded Cuba from that treaty, even though Cuba's territory and interests were very much at stake. Pedro had been watching Mario carefully and noticed that something had begun to burn ferociously, steadily, in his eyes.

"The language of that treaty was a lie, too," Mario had said, directing himself at whoever had tentatively come to his defense. "Neither Spain nor France nor Britain resolved the question of piracy. They never wanted to. Unleashed piracy had its advantages among the rogues financed by the very nations intent on pillaging. Piracy always does."

"Cuba was simply one of several theaters, along with Africa and India," the American retorted.

"It wasn't a stage," Mario corrected him. "It was a real place, filled with real people." Mario brought his napkin to his lips, waiting, carefully weighing what he wanted to say.

"That world war those European powers staged from 1744 to 1783, that place where they fought one another for commercial supremacy—it was someone's homeland."

This last word Mario pronounced as if it were two. Pedro remembered watching Mario as he spoke, his hands with their long, tapered fingers cupped in midair, as if he were about to receive some invisible bounty.

Pedro understood now, in hindsight, that it had been a plea Mario was making to them all, a desperately personal one. The moment recalled seemed to arc invisibly in the air, triggering a flash of intuition that let Pedro sense what had happened to Mario in the very last moments of his life, how he must have made that gesture toward his interrogators in those last minutes, extending his hands in that same way, as if to indicate his willingness to take what had been given to him, no matter how bitter or unjust.

"You don't know that, Pedro." Mario's words intruded, shattering Pedro's reverie. "My last moments on this earth. What I said or what I did."

"I know you were right all along," Pedro said, ashamed at the resistance he had carried with him like a weight across the years.

Spain, France, and Britain had fought like rival school-yard bullies, their pockets full of prized marbles. Then they named the islands of the Greater and Lesser Antilles after venerable saints or the Trinity of Father, Son, and Holy Ghost—as if the act of naming would absolve them or sanctify whatever treachery they had committed in the name of God. Did they believe that the possession of the land would justify the brutality of their means? Back and forth went those venerable marbles. Globes of human longing and sorrow crystallized, forgotten, passed from bully to bully: Saint Lucia, Saint Kitts, Saint Vincent, Santo Domingo, Trinidad. Back and forth, back and forth they went, each bully vying to gain ascendancy over the other. In 1492, when the conquering Castilians wrote home, they described Cuba as a beautiful virgin who willingly yielded herself to them.

"You asked the American, you told all of us that day, 'I suppose the crime committed against those poor Indians, like the poor Indians on your continent, wasn't rape? I suppose you'd argue they asked for it?' Do you remember, Mario?"

"That luncheon is long over, Pedro. You survived. Why doesn't that matter to you?"

"I didn't see you again until the following winter, when

your paintings were being displayed, part of a faculty exhibit. I assumed you'd be holding a grudge against me for
having sided with the American. You sent me a handwritten invitation instead. You greeted me like an old
friend."

"I introduced you to Sonya that day. Do you remember?"

Pedro couldn't answer. He turned away, facing the sea
again, choking back tears, reaching for his briefcase,
pushing the corners of the manuscript down as deeply as
he could into its bowels, fidgeting with the broad leather
flap and worn lock.

"You couldn't take your eyes off her."

Pedro could feel the gusting wind pelting him mercilessly with sand. He could smell something rotting, hear
the receding wave, the bright sound of cellophane being
gathered by deft, invisible fingers. A terrible wave of guilt
rose within Pedro, and its crest broke over his heart. The
briefcase slipped from his grasp and struck the sidewalk.
The latch popped open. The yellowed pages of the manuscript began spilling out, their brittle edges snapping and
fluttering in the breeze, the history Pedro had written
pouring from the worn leather case, floating before him in
midair like some strange hieroglyph he could not read.

"Help me," Pedro pleaded as he scrambled awkwardly to catch the pages lifting on the breeze and tumbling along the sidewalk.

"Let them go."

Mario's words coursed through the emaciated cavity that held Pedro's heart. Pedro leaned against the seawall until he felt the fingers of the afternoon sun bracing the muscles under his shoulder blades. He clutched the briefcase Mario and Sonya had given him long ago tightly in his right hand. He could feel the tide of fear retreating, gathering force.

"You keep writing about the interregnum between Batista and Fidel."

"It's safer," Pedro said.

"Safer than what?"

Another wave of anxiety broke over Pedro, as though every idea, every phrase he had ever thought or considered was exploding through his chest, his every word pulverized and buffeted by time.

"It's easier," he said to Mario.

"To lurk with the dead?"

Pedro avoided the question, sinking instead into the sound of the waves striking the seawall at regular intervals, until he could separate one from the other, anticipating the moment when each struck, until the sound of the ocean became the sound of an enormous metronome that caused his thoughts to disperse and gather and disperse again, each time testing his faith in their tensile strength, his ability to gather together these once shattered fragments, gather them together, there, in his mind, on the curling edge of each wave. He found himself tugging mentally at each one, wanting to make it break at a certain moment, coaxing it to crest and form the rhythms that would force the words that slipped past him to appear and stay solidly, perfectly with him, once and for all.

The interval between ebb and flow, the looming space in Pedro's mind, grew broader and deeper and emptier the more he tried to peer inside it. He wanted to tell the truth about the interval between Batista and Fidel; the truth about what had happened between Mario and himself, about who he had been before his detention and what he became afterward. This space was what Pedro longed desperately to fill with words, and so his rising desperation transformed itself into an anxiety that struck him hard across the breast, made him lose his footing and begin tumbling and scraping endlessly against his own ambivalence and malevolence. Pedro looked out at the sweep of the port and the crystalline blue sky and water.

"'I have never seen such a beautiful place,'" Mario whispered.

"You loved to quote Columbus. That line, it became your refrain," Pedro said, looking over at Mario to gauge his response.

"It became yours."

Pedro flinched and raised his shoulders up as high as he could. Something was searching for him again, the beam of a prison guard's torch in the darkness, the promise of some further degradation. Pedro sank into the gauntness of his torso, hoping the guard's beam would pass over him silently. He tried to flatten his flesh into the damp stone, to emulate the heavy weight of sleep and prepare himself not to react to the scurrying rats, agitated by the light of the torch, that skipped like flat pebbles across the prisoners' heads, shoulders, hips. Pedro tried to breathe deeply, to emulate the rhythms of a sleeping man. He could sense the guard passing, noticing nothing unusual, immured by habit from the irrationality of the scene, the human life that lay wasting before him on the ancient fortress floor, the absurdity of his own role. Prisoners and guards—they all seemed to Pedro as one man fused together within the arc of five hundred years.

Later, Pedro was placed in solitary confinement in a dirt bunker barely larger than the span of his arms and legs. There he lay in complete isolation, his ankles and calves crossed over the hole where he evacuated his bowels every day. The involuntary movement of his intestines became a way to keep time in the eternity of isolation—or its obverse, time's frenetic push, an illusion created by the guards, who would bring the prisoners a succession of meals at three-hour intervals and then none at all in order to disorient them even more. He endured for eight months without reference to another human voice, to a patch of light that would connect him to something larger, by listening to Mario whisper.

In that dirt bunker where the guards kept him after each interrogation, listening to the sound of Mario's voice had kept Pedro alive. He would strain to hear Mario's voice, the effort causing him to recede farther from the surface contours of his body and deeper into the grave-like space where his torturers had left him to die, his mind driving him through and past that cold ground and toward a benevolent space where he could imagine and then listen attentively for his friend's rebuttal. Suddenly Mario would be staring at him, whispering, peering out of that darkness that Pedro

CHAPTER THIRTEEN

"¿Donde va la 'Nina?
¿Pidiendo almas en la esquina?
Viejita de mi alma,
Pon algo en mi palma."

Saturnina walked away, leaving Camilo's *aguacatón* behind her. Above the din of the crowd, she could hear the high-pitched voices of the children, how their voices rose, carrying her up toward the sky, then dropped away again, leaving her alone. Turning her face toward the sun, she silently claimed her affinity with everything that dies. She could feel her heartache commingling with the children's rhymes. She listened carefully, the way Tomás had taught her to do. Above the din, she could hear the children's voices, the sounds of the buses and cars, men and women chanting gleefully, angrily, swarming over the sidewalks and streets, the whisper of her son's voice so close to her ears.

"*¡Mamá! ¡Mamá!*"

"*¡Tomás!*"

Saturnina could feel herself sinking to the ground again, the clouds drifting high above her across a piece of sky that lay suspended between buildings.

"*¡Tomás!*"

Her son's voice had disappeared.

"*¡Tomás!*"

"*Viejita*, where're you going?"

Saturnina turned, frightened to see a figure dressed in black. She squinted and made out what appeared to be a woman inhaling and then pushing out great white billows of smoke like some terrible dragon. Her black shirt was knotted under her bosom, revealing her midriff and the waistline of a very short black skirt with a bright red hemline. Saturnina watched her smile, the tufts of the dragon's overbleached hair flattened by a pair of white plastic sunglasses that sat on the top of her head.

"*Me voy al carajo,*" Saturnina retorted, angered by the heat and the noise, by the obvious intent of this woman who began to undergo some sort of metamorphosis, moving her limbs so that she appeared to Saturnina as an enormous spider, there to lure her away from Tomás, to entangle her in the soft cobwebs of doubt that Saturnina had once again begun to feel accumulating in the remote corners of her heart.

"You're going to the devil, old woman? I'll meet you there," the blond snorted, laughing, punctuating her response with a stream of smoke that she pushed through her red, puckered lips.

Saturnina took a few steps forward, the weight of her dusty skirts pulling her downward. Then she turned and walked back to face the blond, who was now resting on the bus-stop bench.

"*Fidel cayó, mijita. Fidel calló.*"

"*Mira, vieja,* you shouldn't tell stories like that."

"He fell from a great height like a royal horse in battle. I can show you the blood."

There was something about the way Saturnina pointed to the stained edges of her skirts, the way her breath defiantly pushed the phlegm of her words up and out, that caused the blond to fear her.

"Don't say that."

Both women were startled by the sound of the *camello* pulling up to the curb, its brakes squealing violently, its tailpipe spewing a long stream of dense, black smoke.

"Even if it's true?" Saturnina shouted, trailing the blond across the street.

The bus was less like a camel in appearance than like a giant brittle caterpillar, a mechanical caravan of old Swedish buses, long past their prime, that had been soldered together. Saturnina watched the blond board and then got on herself. The driver shifted into gear, and the *camello* lurched violently. From her vantage point in the entry well, Saturnina could see the blond almost lose her balance, then push past the men sitting on either side of the aisle, boxing their ears whenever they tried to run their hands up her short skirt. Saturnina had no such difficulty reaching the back of the bus. In those close quarters, the passengers parted with every rustle of her skirts.

"You smell like a goat!" someone shouted.

"*Fidel cayó. Fidel calló.* I told you how he fell from a great height like a royal horse in battle, but you refuse to believe me."

The passengers nearby fell silent.

"I can show you the blood," Saturnina insisted, her attention intent on the blond, who had by now made her way toward someone she seemed to know, a feeble wisp of a girl in long muslin sleeves.

Saturnina began to tell the morning's news, replete with details, the story's pieces connecting one to the other, the filament of cause and effect running through each, its strength magnificent, like the magic that kept the separate parts of the giant bus moving, pitching, swaying as one coherent, unified form.

"I heard it on the street, near the university, this morning," one passenger whispered to another.

"The students were all out on the quad," the girl in the long muslin sleeves offered.

"Conchita, you went to see Camilo, didn't you?" the blond asked.

"Amparo, don't get angry at me," Conchita pleaded, raising the end of a sleeve to her mouth and chewing nervously.

"¿*Amparo*? Shelter? Is that what you are?" Saturnina asked.

"What do you mean, is that what I am?" Amparo scowled.

"What if I did try to see Camilo?" Concha pleaded.

"My love life is none of your business, Concha."

"You're my *amparo*, then. Here to comfort and assist me. My son sent you. He knew it might be too much." Tears of gratitude welled up in Saturnina's eyes.

Saturnina watched Amparo's friend chew nervously on the end of her sleeve. The dark circles under the girl's eyes and the narrow shoulders she held close to her ears made her appear old and fragile. A strange quiet had fallen over all the passengers. Only the roar of the engine, the brakes squealing, the gears grinding every time the driver shifted, could be heard. Saturnina looked at Amparo, the sunglasses clipped to her damp, swelling cleavage, whatever losses she had experienced clearly written across her face. The passengers were all pressed tightly together in the heat, rocking and swaying like a single rider lurching across waves of desert sand dunes, each movement echoing the broken pavement of the street. When the driver swerved to avoid a pothole, one of the men lurched forward and found nothing to brace his fall except Amparo's buttocks. Without hesitation, she turned and punched him in the face.

"What's the matter with you?" Amparo demanded. "You're men enough to grab a piece of ass. That's about it. What the hell are you doing here? Have you forgotten how to be men?"

Saturnina could see the rage in Amparo's face. She could sense the dark undertow pulling Amparo down into its depths, and she sought to comfort the one Tomás had sent to assist her.

"*Fidel cayó, mijita. Fidel calló.* He silenced, and then he fell from a great height like a royal horse in battle. I can show you the blood."

"You expect me to believe that?" Conchita asked.

"Yes," Saturnina insisted.

"What if it is true?" Amparo asked.

"Make sure everyone knows," Saturnina said. "You want to find Camilo, don't you? He must have hurt you, Amparo, the way he hurt me."

"Maybe I hurt him," Amparo retorted. She held on to the rail with one hand. The other hand she cupped to her mouth.

"*¡Fidel calló!*" Amparo shouted.

"*¡Fidel cayó, mijita, y Fidel calló!*" Saturnina added.

"Wha'd the old bat say?" one of the passengers sitting directly behind the driver asked.

"He fell from a great height like a royal horse in battle," Saturnina roared.

"She wears a saddle?"

"No one's saddled that one for a while." The driver laughed and swerved violently to miss a pedestrian.

"She went into battle, you moron," another passenger called out. "She must be a veteran."

"I can show you the blood," Saturnina bellowed.

"Didn't I tell you? She was wounded."

"Yeah, in the battle of Dos Rios," a man squeezed near a sealed window said.

The passengers roared with laughter.

"Hey, show some respect."

"She's out of her head, poor thing."

"Wounded in the head," the driver snorted, twirling his right forefinger near his temple.

Then he pulled the bus over. He wanted to get to the bottom of the commotion before he had a more difficult problem on his hands. He stood up, pushed his cap back from his forehead, and addressed Saturnina, who was still standing at the back of the bus.

"*¡Silencio! ¡Silencio!*" the driver demanded. "*Vieja*, what did you say?"

Saturnina paused and looked at the driver, shaping her words carefully, patiently, aware of the eerie silence, as if a wave of skepticism had allowed itself to be drawn back farther than anyone thought possible. She placed each word within the span of that silence, addressing the driver the way she would a child who didn't understand:

"*Fidel cayó y Fidel calló.*"

"That's not possible," the driver said.

"Here is the blood that poured from the brothers' wounds."

Most of the passengers couldn't see the edges of Saturnina's skirts, but her words seemed to churn and roar, rapidly sweeping over them, inundating every possible doubt or hesitation. Women began weeping and wailing. Some people cried out for God's mercy. Others were paralyzed with fear.

"Here's the blood!" Saturnina shouted above the din of voices.

"Get me off this damn bus," one of the men demanded.

"We want to get home."

"We want to get off the bus."

The driver threw the lever that opened the doors. Most of the passengers, terrified, rushed toward the exits, pushing everyone before them. Saturnina grabbed a nearby rail and watched as Conchita and Amparo, who were standing closer to the rear door well, were swept out by the frantic passengers. The driver, visibly shaken, said nothing. He sat down, slammed the doors shut, engaged the clutch, and shifted into first gear.

"¡*Fidel calló!*" a young man shouted, leaning his torso out one of the windows that still worked.

"¡*Fidel calló!*" someone else repeated, leaning out another window and allowing his anxiety to become glee.

Saturnina looked through the *camello*'s rear window, cloudy with dust and the residue of tailpipe fumes, and caught sight of Amparo, her arm protectively encircling Conchita as if the two women were mother and child.

"Look," Saturnina insisted, shaking the shoulder of a woman sitting nearby crying, paralyzed in fear. "Look."

The remaining passengers turned and saw what belonged to them all. The image began to distill itself into each of their hearts as something that had to be vindicated. The *camello* pitched and turned through the city streets, every movement rocking them awake, releasing them from their fearful dream. At the next stop, Saturnina stepped off before the *camello* headed along the broad avenue to the suburbs of Miramar. She knew the passengers would retell the tale, adding their own doubts and wishes, emphasizing one or another detail, the way any ancient storyteller would. Though she would have been hard-pressed to explain it, she knew that the long-faded desires traced invisibly into the consciousness of every generation had awakened in the press and roll of the bus, the press and roll of the story the passengers had overheard first that morning in their errands around the city and then later between Amparo and Conchita. Those desires had now brought them back to the subterranean vein of a faith they had known in childhood but had long forgotten.

Not much later in the day, they would all step out into the streets—in protest, in despair, in solidarity, or perhaps driven by a curiosity about what change might feel like. Whatever the motivation, it would become possible for them to leap over the reef they had allowed to form around them. Once on the other side of that barrier, nothing could withstand the force of their bodies and voices and hopes pressing in from the suburbs toward La Plaza de la Revolucíon. Reminded by the angry Amparo's taunt about a possibility they could barely remember, reinforced by the image of the two young women embracing as mother and child, riding pushcarts and wheelbarrows, bicycles and mopeds, all of them would be drawn into the city like a noisy tide by the force of a beckoning moon.

CHAPTER FOURTEEN

"It's time." Mario whispered.

Pedro let his gaze settle on the gulls that were gliding across the sky, the grace of the arcs they formed, the interplay of muscle and bone against the pressure of the air that both sustained them and pressed them downward. The seawall felt cold and hard to him, even in the afternoon sun. Pedro checked his wristwatch. It was almost three o'clock.

"It must seem impossible now."

"What's that, Mario?"

"To believe you can move toward anything."

Pedro looked around. In the horror of detention he had learned to stop time by lying as still as possible, and a part of him had even come to believe that prolonged physical stillness could render him invisible. The deeper he retreated from the surface of his skin and into the recesses of his memory, the safer he believed himself to be.

"It's time, Pedro."

Pedro began walking east along the avenue, Mario at his side. For Pedro, the choice was intuitive. To walk east was to walk into the past, to embrace Guantánamo, a piece of land taken by guile, at the tip of a U.S. rifle, but a piece that belonged to him nevertheless, even now. Nothing changed. It was all the same moment, the same history again and again. Under capitalist or communist banner, the powerful rationalized greed and violence. The earth was soaked in blood, every stone wall saturated with the cries of the innocent. The eastern tip of Cuba was stolen, turned into a foreign military base, a prison chamber as repulsive as anything Batista or Fidel ever devised.

Pedro slowed to a halt, facing Mario.

"I said your name. I killed you."

"You were tortured within an inch of your life, Pedro."

"I was too afraid to help you."

"We were all afraid, Pedro."

"You did what was right anyway."

"I did what was mine to do."

Pedro looked down, a strange smile, half grimace, crossing his face.

"One of the political prisoners I did time with, Joselito, was so much like you. 'He is as fearless as Mario,' I kept telling myself. I couldn't believe it was possible. Every day, when the guards weren't looking, Joselito would pick up every strip of palm frond he could find and hide it in his clothes. Every night, he would tap the rhythms of old *boleros* against his cell wall. We gathered for work detail one morning, and a young *campesino* with a neck as wide as a bull's took Joselito's place in formation. That's how we knew. Rodrigo told us later how the two guards on morgue duty had cut Joselito's body down and thrown it into a ditch just a few miles from the prison. 'Didn't wrap him up or anything,' Rodrigo kept saying. I started to dream of Joselito's body in a lime-spattered ditch. I dreamed of your body and Joselito's tangled together for eternity."

"It's over." Mario placed his arms around Pedro's shoulders to lessen the old man's sobs.

"Rodrigo kept a piece of the palm fronds Joselito had braided into a cord and wrapped around his neck. He didn't want to forget, he said. I remember wondering, how could you possibly forget? By the time Rodrigo found me, after his release, the braid was dry and brittle. It reminded me of the palm fronds the ruddy-faced parish priest in Remedios would bless and give away every year on Palm Sunday, the same ones my mother would fasten into the shape of a cross and save. I couldn't stop thinking: The green palm sheaves that cushioned the prophet's passage into the holy city, and the sheaves Joselito stripped and tucked under his clothes when no one was looking—what was the difference?"

Pedro mopped his face with his handkerchief.

"Mario, you were just like Joselito. You chose your death, and so defined your life, riding your idealism into the fray, a mimeograph machine your broken lance."

"What happened to the other prisoners?"

Pedro shrugged, trying to shift the weight of his memories off his shoulders.

"Manfredis and Rodrigo were released after eleven years. They both came to see me, but I was so afraid of the block spies I tried to hide. Sonya went downstairs to welcome them. She opened the apartment building door wide and waved to the neighbors peering between their curtains."

The pain in Pedro Valle's chest began to ebb, the scent of sea foam and gardenias to flow, as the memory of Sonya washed over him. She was wearing her wedding dress, an orchid in her hair, which she had pulled back onto the nape of her neck in a thick, dark chignon. She was wearing white satin, gliding down the aisle toward Mario, who stood at the altar waiting expectantly, Pedro, his best man, beside him. To Pedro, she appeared liquid, as if water the color and luminosity of a pearl were cascading over her, undulating, shimmering in time with the smallest movement of her body.

"Isn't it time to remember truthfully, Pedro?"

Pedro stopped. "You're blocking my path east. I'm an old man, for heaven's sake. Let me pass."

"Tell the truth."

Pedro looked away, unable to sustain Mario's gaze.

"It was the heat of the sun, Mario. That's why I got up and went swimming."

"Tell me."

"I was sick and tired of your Marxist harangue, so I went swimming."

"I was never a Marxist."

"No, you weren't. You were actually the first person I heard say that Fidel would align himself with the Soviets in response to U.S. ultimatums. I'm sorry. You were right, Mario. I was wrong. I didn't recognize it, didn't want to, that day on the beach."

Pedro smiled sadly, thinking about the earnest expression on Mario's face that day when he had accused Pedro

of forgetting his own history. It was on one of those out-
ings Sonya organized with the help of whoever Pedro was
seeing at the time. Patricia? Or was it Graciela, the one
who looked so much like Edith Piaf? "You're dating a
sparrow," Mario had teased him. And there it was, that
something in Pedro's eye that revealed how infatuated he
was with Sonya. Pedro knew Mario had seen it. They
were all lounging on a beach somewhere, on blankets and
deck chairs, a group of colleagues and their wives on a
congenial summer outing. Yet when Pedro couldn't bear
Mario's opinions anymore, when he had no further rebuttal, he had simply gotten up and walked into the sea.
'You've forgotten your own history,' Mario had called out
to him.

Pedro had bristled, but now he understood that Mario's
words had pointed toward something more difficult that
lay deep within Pedro, unexcavated, despite his time as a
political prisoner. Remembering how Mario had accused
him of forgetting, how Mario had selected and strung
together the facts and told the story of Cuba in a way that
mesmerized all his listeners, made Pedro feel restless,
compelled to put down on paper the truth of his betrayal
of Mario. The massive, churning stream he had watched
silently for so long was beckoning to him again.

Pedro remembered rising angrily from his beach chair, walking into the sea, and swimming away until he could forget the look on Sonya's face, the intensity, the love with which she had spent the afternoon listening to Mario telling Cuba's history in a way that Pedro never could. Even after Mario's disappearance, after she had married Pedro, she never looked at him in the same way she had looked at Mario that day.

Pedro fell silent as he and Mario continued walking east. Memories of their quarrelsome day at the beach broke over the mental barriers he had set so firmly in place. He remembered the little sparrow's hands that evening at dinner. They were too frail, the web of blue veins too prominent. Earlier, when he had returned exhausted from his long swim, it was the little sparrow who had told him, smiling, her hands the wings of a dying butterfly, that Sonya was taking a walk along the beach with Mario, that they had been gone for a long time. When Pedro saw Sonya in the hotel lobby, he hung back behind a pillar, as if by watching the surface of this thing he loved so much he could learn something of its impossible fidelity to Mario. She seemed so happy to Pedro, happier than he could ever make her. As Pedro watched her and Mario walking arm in arm into the hotel restaurant and greeting the other couples, there was one certainty in Pedro's mind: She loved Mario.

At dinner, Mario, pugnacious and charming, his face flushed with wine and candlelight, seemed to be looking pointedly at Pedro. "A man who treats his neighbor charitably tends to welcome that neighbor's retaliation in kind," he had said. "A man who steals fears theft." It was as if the dapper man Pedro had first observed at the faculty dining hall had appeared before him again, only now Pedro was playing the unenviable role of the American. Now Mario was telling all of them, especially the wives who sat rapt in their seats staring languidly at him, crossing and uncrossing their legs, his thesis on American slavery and how Franklin Pierce, one of its fervent advocates, had won the U.S. presidential election of 1852 by a landslide.

"They all wanted slavery," Mario had insisted. "The public, the politicians. Why call it by another name or talk instead about economics or moral progress? Pierce's ministers to Spain, France, and England drew up the Ostend Manifesto, recommending the purchase of Cuba. But who decided we were up for sale?"

Every word Mario spoke seemed to be spoken for Sonya and infused with a meaning only the two of them could discern. "'If we do not purchase Cuba now, Pierce's ministers warned, the island will be '"Africanized."'" If Spain doesn't want to sell Cuba, the U.S. would be justified in taking it. If our neighbor's house was on fire and the flames might eventually reach us, we would be morally justified in tearing down his home first. Not one of them had the courage to question the equation of blackness with a fire that would leave their property and their white skins charred. They feared the slaves' retaliation because they feared the very conditions they had created and then institutionalized."

"Profit over people. Is that your point?" Pedro interrupted, shrugging dismissively.

He remembered Mario pausing, blowing the smoke slowly through his lips before speaking. "The point, Pedro, is that Cuba was no longer a piece of fruit, *la fruta madura*, ripe for consumption. It was a house burning, its fires threatening an ever more horrific blackening of property and of self. They had found a better metaphor, one that used fear to coalesce xenophobia and jingoism, to rationalize greed, to turn the basest emotions into preemptive action. The world needs those who stake themselves against the refusal to attach facts to meaning, all of which amounts to willful amnesia."

Pedro spoke without sensing how angry he was. "What is it you think I've forgotten, Mario? Do you think you know that history better than I do? You're a painter." Pedro's words lingered and expanded in his mouth unpleasantly, and he could see the anger flashing palpably across Mario's face.

"When you can't bear my arguments, when you have no reasonable response, you call me a painter." Then Mario flashed his charismatic smile. Everyone laughed, sitting back gratefully into their chairs. Everyone drank their glasses to the dregs and beckoned to the waiters for more.

An enormous wave crashed against the seawall. Pedro, an old man now, turned to face the sea, reaching with one arm for the wall's broad ledge and forcing himself to lean forward toward the very thing he feared most.

"You were in love with Sonya."

Pedro released the ledge and clutched the worn briefcase, extending it before him as if it were a shield that would help him ward off the blows of the truncheon, incessant, powerful, knocking the breath out of him.

"I couldn't bear how much she loved you, Mario. Not me, you."

"Is that why you didn't stand with me?"

Pedro could feel the heat of the afternoon sun sinking

deep into his bones as he tried to press forward, walking east along El Malecón, the Caleta de San Lazaro on his left. In the distance, on one side of El Malecón, he could see the Castillo de San Salvador de la Punta. On the other side was the entrance to El Parque de los Martires, which seemed to beckon to him.

"I'm tired, Mario. I need to sit."

"Cuba is like a woman beaten by a succession of violent men, corrupted by a desire that has brooked all contradictions. Do you remember me telling you that, Pedro?"

"I remember telling you it's a choice she makes."

"Pedro, why does a wife endure her husband's violence?"

"Because she still loves him."

"Love has nothing to do with it."

"What, then?"

"Because she can't imagine anything else," Mario said. "Neither can you."

Pedro fell silent for a moment. "So nothing ever changes," he said, looking over at his friend.

"No, not until she imagines something else, something better."

CHAPTER FIFTEEN

"Saturnina, estate tranquila.
No busques problemas con las vecinas.
Cuando te pregunten
Habla la verdad.
Cuando se angustien
Corre con velocidad."

How those unbelieving passengers suffered. What did they expect? Saturnina wondered. For wasn't that the problem with this world—that everything was delayed because of unbelief? How could her son be expected to return to this place where no one believed the most literal testament? Batista silenced and Batista fell; Fidel silenced and Fidel fell. Batista killed her son. Fidel delayed her son's return. Brutality and unbelief—how those chains could wrap around our necks and pull us down into dark waters. The thought made Saturnina aware of the weight of her skirts, how they could pull her into and under the waters that held no promise of salvation. A wave of fear overcame Saturnina. She reached into her pouch of tesserae and pulled one out. She squatted on the ground. Right to left, she drew a circle in the dirt with her bit of mosaic. She must fear nothing. The circle was complete. Her son would return. She had been a witness. The very edges of her skirts bore traces of the material truth of her words. The old woman once again turned her face toward the afternoon sky; the air was moist, heavy with heat.

"*El volverá*," she whispered to herself, clenching her lids shut in prayer. "My son shall return."

The thought occurred to her in that instant that perhaps the fault was hers. That if she had listened to Tomás more closely, had believed more purely, had paced more precisely around the statue of La Milagrosa, had not stopped to help Camilo, then Tomás would have returned already. She must have done something wrong, though the heavens must know it was not what she had intended. She had been given the task of heralding her son's return, yet she had not been completely without doubt.

"*¡Basta!*" She would again announce his arrival, and she would do it with even more fervor.

Saturnina's mind drifted to the memory of her son's body. The gunshot that had left a gaping hole in his chest had left her vacant, too. And so she had decided to live here in these streets after Vania's betrayal, for she could never have witnessed the sign of Tomás's return if she had been at home.

The *camello* had dropped her off only a few blocks from the apartment she once had shared with Vania and Tomás and later with Vania and Pablo. Saturnina had conferred with the trees and birds; had spoken to La Milagrosa; had tried to help her sad Camilo, who had returned to drive her across the city in his sea-monster-green taxi; had witnessed the spider's conversion into a believing woman. Now it was clear: What Tomás wanted was for her to return to the home he had shared with Vania. He wanted her to rescue Vania so that they could all be together again.

When she arrived in front of the building, she looked up toward the once familiar balcony and saw a fat bundle of a man sitting in a chair snoring heavily, his head thrown back to reveal the cave of his mouth.

"*¿Pablo? ¡Pablo! ¡Despiertate, Pablo!*"

Eventually Saturnina's words did pierce the cloud of rum that enveloped him, though she managed as well to bring the neighbors who still remained home that day to the crevice of every doorway, window, and balcony. Startled awake, an aged Pablo leaned over the balcony, his glasses slipping to the tip of his greasy nose, and discovered Saturnina, who was at first unrecognizable to him.

"What are you doing here? I thought you were dead, old woman."

"¡FIDEL CAYÓ, PABLO! ¡FIDEL CALLÓ!"

"Shhhhhh—be quiet. Are you crazy?"

"Despiertate borracho y mira la verdad," she thundered at him like a minister from a pulpit. But by calling him a drunk and demanding that he awaken to the truth of her words, Saturnina only angered Pablo.

"What do you want?" he hissed at her over the balcony rail.

"Fidel has silenced, and Fidel has fallen," she bellowed, raising her arms and shaking both arthritic hands at Pablo and his neighbors.

"Be quiet, you stupid old woman. You could get all of us in a lot of trouble."

"¡FIDEL CAYÓ Y FIDEL CALLÓ!"

Pablo's neighbors peered out at this miserly man who had never, in all their years of living side by side, had a kind word or gesture for any of them. They began to wonder how they might profit from his obvious misfortune, how they could use the old beggar-woman's words to denounce him to the authorities or simply ridicule him.

"We never knew you had counterrevolutionary friends, Pablo," Ester jeered at him from one of the balconies across the street, herself only slightly less haggard and hungry than Saturnina.

"Shut up," Pablo snapped over the howls of laughter. He turned and slammed the balcony door behind him.

"*¡FIDEL CAYÓ Y FIDEL CALLÓ!*" Saturnina shouted, afraid her message would get lost in the animosity among neighbors.

"*Oye, vieja,*" Ester called down to her, "I've been hearing that all day. It's not really true. Is it?"

It was as if everyone in that split instant between Ester's question and Saturnina's response was suspended between cynicism and hope, despair and laughter.

"*Sí. Fidel calló,*" Saturnina repeated, not loudly this time but almost in a whisper, hoarse and earnest. She knew that she had little time left to convert them all to the truth that she knew, the truth that would bring her son home.

"How could that be?" a neighbor called out to her.

"How could that be?" Saturnina echoed. "I saw it with

my own eyes. When the heavens open up and blaze with fire, do you question the time? I tell you I saw Fidel, standing at a great height, fall to the cobblestones we common people tread every day. I saw what was left of him afterward. The pieces the people carried away. The blood."

Here Saturnina paused, remembering that she carried the evidence of Fidel's fall with her.

"Look!" She raised the edges of her skirt delicately, as if she were handling a holy shroud.

The crowd that had formed all around her needed no further proof.

"*¡Dios mio! ¡Fidel calló!*" one of the women standing closest to Saturnina confirmed, swooning.

"Yes, and he will return."

"Not if we can help it," Ester shouted at Saturnina over her shoulder.

"He will return. He will return," Saturnina called out after her and the elderly men and women who were shuffling into the street.

The bricks and cobblestones seemed to vibrate with the news as each neighbor scurried along the street. Saturnina watched the very old and the very young stream into the street, plastic toys and pots and ladles in hand, all of them heading toward some mysterious center. The street was eerily empty. Every window and balcony had been shuttered. The neighbors' noisy embarkation for La Plaza de la Revolucíon had left behind only a resounding silence.

Fidel's final exhalation had brought them all to life, infusing them with spirit and purpose, as if all of them together were one body reanimated, galvanized, rising to meet the new day. Too many, she worried, had retreated indoors, huddling in their homes, hunched over radios, searching however they could for the day's news, and thinking about what they had already lost and whatever remained for them to lose. There they sat among the ruins of the crumbling city thinking—amidst broken pipes and broken plaster, in interior courtyards, every stone ringed with weeds, every pillar buckling. There they withdrew to count the hours until their emancipation, wondering who would come to their rescue, waiting the way children wait to be picked up and carried over some frightening obstacle.

It seemed to Saturnina that she had been left alone with her news and her memories and the fears that she, too, held shuttered in her heart. In her confusion, she turned to ask the nearest tree what she should do, to find a bird that might open the path before her, but no bird flitted by to offer its counsel. The palm trees were ominously silent, their fronds suspended in midair. The cap of bright green trees she could see in the near distance seemed miles away. Her sad Camilo and his taxi were nowhere to be found.

The old woman sank onto the front steps of the building she had lived in for so many years and tried to ask the ghosts sweeping past her. They appeared before her on the sidewalk, nodding, smiling, talking to one another as they had in life, except that they didn't seem to hear her. Saturnina's upstairs neighbor, Teresa, appeared and sat down next to her on the steps to drink the dainty demitasse of strong coffee Vania always brought out for them on a turquoise Bakelite tray, the dutiful Vania always calling out behind her, "You dears enjoy your chat," as if she were serving two little girls playing at tea party. Saturnina had been in the habit of turning back in gratitude to wave her thanks to Vania, but today she realized that Tomás was right. The greatest thanks she could give her daughter-in-law would be to save her from Pablo.

As the thought reasserted itself, the vision of a broad swath of ground opened up before her and Vania and extended far into a sunlit horizon, and Saturnina knew again that Tomás was speaking to her. So she got up abruptly, leaving the ghostly and garrulous Teresa behind, and followed what she was certain was her daughter-in-law, turquoise tray in hand, disappearing into the darkness on the other side of the lobby door.

CHAPTER SIXTEEN

★

PEDRO REACHED the entrance to El Parque de los Martires, the monument to the medical students who were murdered on November 27th, 1871, by the Spanish colonial government. The monument seemed to quiver in the bright sunlight, recalling the moment earlier that day when he was about to cross Calle 27 de Noviembre, and the feeling that he wasn't living his own life. He had left his life on the floor of a prison like so much excrement flowing from organs, muscles that had had their innate physical rhythms beaten out of them. His jailors had separated him from himself. The beatings, the humiliation of standing naked and blindfolded for hours, the terror of the mock executions, the hunger that never left him, the sleep perpetually driven away; they had changed him.

In order to endure, he had left himself behind. Wasn't that his greater humiliation? Hadn't that been his tormentors' victory? They had started to think of him as a psychiatric case, forever talking to someone invisible; wasn't that why they had lifted him into the transport van and dropped him onto a city sidewalk?

"You won. You survived," Sonya told him repeatedly, and he would look at her, barely able to recognize the woman he had married, the lines around her mouth, the dark shadows under her eyes, the gray streaks in her hair. How could he explain to this stranger who now lay beside him every night that it was not an act of contrition, of mercy or exhaustion that led his tormentors to release him, but an opportunity for propaganda? He had become an object lesson against dissent and for the innate corruptibility of the bourgeoisie. To survive, he had split himself in two; the body tortured and the mind that pulled far up into itself in order to find the solace of a thread of narrative, the trace of a memory, like a song about a landscape he had crossed but no one else could find on a map, refused even to believe existed.

He had spoken Mario's name and left his own life in

that interrogation room. Whoever had risen from that stone floor wasn't the same man who had entered the room, no matter the adequacy with which he had learned again to move through his days. It was an act of mimicry, this trying to remember whom he had been or could have become in any single moment.

"I envy them, Mario." Pedro let his eyes rest on the monument to the eight young medical students who had become martyrs to Cuban nationalism.

"Why is that?"

"Their deaths rendered them whole. They would have disappeared otherwise into the dark abyss of time."

Pedro could imagine them, so full of life and ambition, walking through San Antonio Chiquito, a cemetery that no longer existed, assigned to gather the human cadavers necessary for their studies in anatomy. It must have been a gruesome task, even in the glare of white marble on a tropical noon, warm even in January. Which of those eight boys had been the first to find respite in humor? he wondered. Which had nervously shoved a companion, triggering shouts and peals of laughter? Then that last playful shove, the one that caused one of them to bump against the wooden cart stacked with paupers' bodies, the cart almost tipping, coming close or perhaps actually scraping against the tomb of the recently deceased Spanish general, Don Castañón.

That playful gesture altered the entire trajectory of their lives. They would have all become country doctors and lived quietly to some reasonable old age if Wenceslao de Villaurrutia hadn't been standing in the cemetery that day, his jealous heart enraged. Villaurrutia was relentless, insisting that the medical students' horseplay was, not only disrespectful, but an obviously political affirmation of Cuban national identity by a group of revolutionary thugs, dead-enders with neither prospect nor hope. He argued that their actions, on sanctified ground, before the sepulcher dedicated to the patriotic Spanish volunteers who served in the colonial militia, and in the very niche where the remains of their General Castañón lay, could have no other interpretation.

Pedro thought about how Villaurrutia's rage had dovetailed into the political calculations of the island's Spanish Governor, Dionisio López Roberts, who saw in the public reaction to the students' gesture an opportunity to consolidate his reputation with the Spanish patriots on the island and those back home in Spain. It was an opportunity to make a lot of money, too—through extortion, because the more students he detained in response to Villaurrutia's uncorroborated claim, the greater the number of parents who would be eager to pay him under the table for their sons' release.

It occurred to Pedro as he stood looking at the statue that his own gesture of getting up and walking into the sea that day long ago had revealed to both Sonya and Mario the depth of the insecurity that raged within him, the sense that he could only ever be unloved. After that summer outing, Sonya never trusted him again in quite the same way, never shared her thoughts with him without first winnowing away whatever might cause him the slightest unease. He had blamed Mario, but wasn't there another way of seeing what had happened?

"What if I had never gotten up and walked away, Mario?"

"Which time?"

Pedro could feel Mario's words striking him across the chest. The old man sat down on a bench near the statue to catch his breath.

"Every time, Mario. Every single time I walked away and you forgave me. If I had never walked away, then what?"

Pedro turned to observe Mario in profile. Mario's gaze seemed to be touching the statue's surface, as though he were searching for an answer to Pedro's question.

Other memories that had lain beyond Pedro's grasp for so many years began to rise to the surface, and he could feel panic surging up from his belly to his throat. He thought about the moment when, just a year before Sonya and Mario married, he had accidentally discovered the drawings Mario had made of her. Pedro's body had shaken with anger, and yet he had felt a fathomless hollow within himself. He could find nothing in the infinite silence the drawings had pushed him into, no tears, only a dizzying emptiness, an abyss of feeling held open by the buzz and rattle of his nerves across his skin.

That day, while Sonya chatted away in another room with Graciela and a group of mutual friends, Pedro tucked the drawings back between the blank leaves of Sonya's sketchbook, returned the sketchbook to its remote location at the very top of the closet, hidden from sight, and put a hatbox on top of the sketchbook, exactly as it had been before he had inadvertently disturbed it.

"Did you find the photo albums?" Sonya asked him when he reentered the living room empty-handed.

"I looked and couldn't see them. I didn't want to pry," Pedro said.

"Don't be silly."

"Do you want me to get them?" Mario asked.

"I'll get them."

Sonya returned with two large photo albums that she and her guests began paging through, reminiscing over cups of sweet black tea.

Pedro could not ask Sonya when those drawings had been made, though he did scan each one carefully, front and back, for a trace of a date, an indication. He never asked the question that burned within him: whether his sense of the intimacy, revealed so clearly to him in the drawings, was as real to the artist and its sitter.

The following day, he went to confront Mario and found him standing at his easel, a model on the dais he himself had built. For several moments, before he actually saw the model's face, Pedro believed it was Sonya. The model, naked, drenched in the afternoon light that flooded through the open skylights, was startled into modesty less by Pedro's arrival than by his stare. The moment forever afterward would come to Pedro in splinters of sound. His voice felt uncontainable in his

own throat, the expansion of sound offering him no solace in its release, only the acknowledgment of a terrible
wound.

"You've touched her!" he shouted, gasping for air as if
he were drowning in his own rage.

Mario looked at him, his eyes placid, his voice plaintive.
"Who?"

"You know I mean Sonya."

"What's the matter with you, Pedro?"

"The drawings—"

"I'm a painter, Pedro. I've made a lot of drawings."

"Of her."

"Why would you care, Pedro? She's marrying me—
not you."

"You're engaged?"

"Why should you care?" Mario repeated.

Afterward, and this was a great source of befuddle-
ment to Pedro, Mario never mentioned the moment to
Sonya, though eventually Pedro came to interpret that
silence not as a sign of respect or loyalty to himself but as
Mario's desire to protect Sonya.

The event became a ponderous weight within Pedro,
something that would eventually break the surface tension

of his friendship with Mario. It had caused a nearly irreparable breach between them, which Mario had tried to overlook by asking Pedro to be his best man. Pedro had tried to forget, tried his best to let his heart mend. It was Mario's way.

When Mario walked through the doors of the café, what had he expected in return from Pedro? Had he forgotten what had passed between them? Had he believed that the political moment could be greater than the barely dormant jealousy in Pedro's breast, the rivalry that had driven the breach with Mario? Time had proven Mario right—on both counts, political and personal. For the Fidelistas who opposed Batista's oppression had become oppressive themselves; and in fact, in retrospect, Pedro found himself battling chimeras of his own making, turning over and over again in his mind accusations he had never managed to substantiate. Decades later, in the silence that followed Mario's disappearance and Pedro's years as a political prisoner, the question had the substance of a flake of ash.

It was Sonya who came to visit him at the clinic. It was Sonya who picked him up when the doctors released him, bundled him up, and took him to her apartment.

Pedro was now the picture of the reeducated bourgeoisie. He sat neatly dressed on the living room sofa in
trousers and freshly pressed *guayabera*, the coffee table
before him displaying an assortment of glasses and
cups and a tray piled high with Jorge's tiny fruit *empana-
das*, a gift from the neighbor who had scooped him up
off the sidewalk like a half-empty sack. Pedro watched
himself interact with neighbors, friends, and family
members, retreating into his mind, rising to a distant
corner of the room to watch himself, as if it were all a
scene in a play about a man who had been raised from the
dead.

Pedro could still hear the dull tap of glasses and cups
as all those neighbors and friends raised a glass of rum or
sweetened coffee, ate a delicately wrought *empanada*,
all genuinely wishing him well in this second life, all
avoiding the matter of what had been done to him and
why, telling him instead the story of what Sonya had endured in the absence of her husband and her husband's
best friend because it was easier to discuss what they
knew than to wonder what had become of Mario and to
imagine what Pedro had endured in one of Fidel's
prisons.

I don't blame you, Pedro wanted to tell them. I understand. But he was too far away for them to hear. They had come to help him by offering the story of how Sonya spent the months immediately after his arrest traveling from one municipal police station to another, begging for news of Mario and him and being met with either silence or the threat of violence. How the well-wishers had either waited in the car for her during those terrible errands or been nearly arrested themselves for spitting out curses at whichever officer happened to be on duty. In unison they raised their glasses and tapped the rims together gently in praise of Sonya, who had endured with such fidelity the absence of the two men she loved. When all the guests had left, Sonya proposed to him. He was a broken man, but she couldn't bear to be alone, she told him. And Pedro knew what she meant: He was as close as she could be to Mario now. Pedro accepted. They had a civil ceremony a week later. No one was invited.

Mario had been a better friend to Pedro than he had ever been to anyone, including Sonya. The countless kind gestures, moments when Mario had helped him with a friendly word, the reassurance of his presence, nearly overwhelmed Pedro now as he sat on a bench in the Park of the Martyrs waiting for the answers to the questions he had asked Mario so many times in so many different ways.

"I walked away. I betrayed you, Mario, and in return, you forgave me. If I had never walked away, who would I have been? What would have become of me?"

CHAPTER SEVENTEEN

"Saturnina, alma adamantina,
Recuerda el mundo es fango y lagrimas.
Mateo nos dice
(y es la verdad)
El mundo tiene lobos
Feroz cantidad."

Once inside the building, Saturnina wondered where Vania had gone so quickly. She hadn't expected to climb the stairs to their third-floor apartment, but she owed her son and her daughter-in-law this effort. Knowing Pablo would keep her from seeing Vania, she hesitated outside the apartment door. She could hear someone inside. She turned the doorknob and entered, passing through the living and dining rooms, making her way carefully toward the sound. The door that had once separated the kitchen from the dining room was gone, and Saturnina found herself face-to-face with Pablo, who was cutting something on the kitchen counter.

"Get out of here, you smelly cat," he shouted at her, visibly shocked to see anyone in his home but doubly affected to see that it was Saturnina.

"I came to see Vania, not you."

"Vania?"

"You've been beating her again."

"You're out of your mind, *vieja*."

"Where is she?"

"You don't even know what year it is."

The words struck Saturnina as efficiently as a pair of fists. She sank into the chair by the kitchen entrance, her hand over her throat, as if to steady her breath.

"Listen to me, old woman."

Pablo lunged toward her, wanting to drive her out of the apartment, but Saturnina dodged him, fear propelling her across the kitchen. Her fingers touched the handle of the knife he had left lying on the counter and wrapped themselves around it. She raised the knife before her, its long thick blade pointing downward.

Pablo stood opposite her, overweight and haggard, his teeth bared in a terrible snarl, his hands beckoning eagerly, daring her to try to strike him with the knife. Saturnina wanted to do exactly as Pablo asked. She could feel the knife clenched in her fist. She was sure now he was the force that had initiated the devastating chain reaction she had come to think of simply as her life. Every sorrow she had endured since the death of her son drew itself into a sharp, terrible point ready to meet its mark. When she made herself look at Pablo again, though, she sensed something beyond the bared teeth and the swagger, neither of which concealed from her his fear of life's unpredictability and betrayals.

"Still drunk."

"Not a drop. Word of honor," he said, baring his teeth like a crocodile, shaking his head from side to side.

Saturnina had borne witness to this kind of scene many times. Pablo's alcoholism, like his disaffection for Vania and the old woman, had blossomed gradually, its distinct stages marked by moments of varying cruelty. Late in 1962, when the American with his bundles of cash was already a fading memory, Pablo's penury began to ripen, a complement to his depression, a deepening sense of a life unlived, lying just beyond the grasp of his imagination. He started to take his own bottle of rum with him to family gatherings, where he would sit alone, brooding, his fingers wrapped tightly around the bottle's neck, never offering anyone a glass.

The morning Vania had the temerity to ask him where he had been all night, Pablo, the very pores of his skin exuding the stench of alcohol, replied with his fists, beating her for the very first time. After that, the beatings started to come more regularly, the tension mounting over months of sullen silences and unexpressed resentments until it was catalyzed by some random event—coffee served in a chipped cup, a tardy supper, an unmade bed. Pablo's emotions would begin to ebb then, almost to the point of tenderness, until once again the weight of his silence shifted, became ominous, an indicator that his rage had started to flow and build toward its inexorable breaking point.

Saturnina was caught in the middle, always trying to help Vania with the household, stepping in physically between her and Pablo until the day he waved a knife in front of Saturnina's face and threatened to kill her. Having found Vania crying on the bathroom floor, her face bloodied and swollen, Saturnina had gone to the kitchen for ice and found Pablo at the stove preparing the sort of beef stew that only he ever seemed to find appetizing. That day long ago, Pablo had turned to look over his shoulder at Saturnina and sneer, his attention drawn back to the pot on the stove.

"Why did you beat your wife?" Saturnina had asked him.

"She slipped and fell in the bathroom. You know how clumsy Vania is."

"You're drunk again."

"You can't speak to me that way. I'm the man of the house."

Saturnina couldn't remember what she had said next, but she remembered how Pablo turned to face her, in his right hand a long, broad kitchen knife, his hatred for her palpable.

"Try it, Pablo. I'm not Vania."

Pablo took a step toward her, slicing the air with the knife, but he lacked conviction in this as in all things. He turned his back to Saturnina, dropped the knife on the counter, and stood hunched, sobbing over the boiling pot of stew.

The scene marked the beginning of the end of Saturnina's life in that house. Vania, who had learned to hold the calculus of her own self-preservation tightly, passively allowed a line to be drawn, invisible and practical, between herself and her mother-in-law. Saturnina came to understand then the void that was Vania—the hesitations and fears, the indecisiveness. Tomás had protected Vania; Pablo offered her the status of being a married woman. Saturnina could offer nothing as tangible. Shortly after that realization, Saturnina put on every article of clothing she owned and pushed away from the couple's apartment and into the streets of Havana.

"Smelly cat. I told you to get out of my house."

"This is my house, Pablo, the house I shared with my son and his wife. Where is she? Tell me."

Saturnina rose from the chair and planted her feet firmly on the cracked linoleum. She clenched the knife's handle, its blade pointing downward, with all the strength she could summon.

"Tell me."

"Get out of my house, you worthless bitch."

Saturnina's whole body was shaking. She could barely speak, paralyzed by the memories of how he had beaten Vania.

"Where is Vania?"

"Long gone, old woman."

"You killed her."

"She jumped on a raft convinced she'd reach Miami. Don't you remember?"

"You beat her to death."

"Smelly cat. She disappeared into the ocean. Vania, the raft, and whoever else was stupid enough to go with her."

Saturnina thought about the timid girl who had married her son and the ocean wave that would have swallowed her and the raft and her companions whole. A terrible sadness overcame her. Vania would never have left, not that way. She never had the physical courage to confront Pablo, much less board a leaky raft with strangers and strike out into the unknown.

"I want you out of here, old woman. I've had enough of you today, of the past, of those shitheads out in the street dreaming again of revolution."

Saturnina looked up at him through the gauze of her cataracts.

"Why did you kill her?"

The quiet way she spoke, the humility contained in the slope of her head and shoulders, caused the foundations of Pablo's narrow world to shift. Since his marriage to Vania in 1958, through every change in circumstance since then, he had reinforced himself with alcohol and the bile of his anger. Now, more than anything else, he wanted to contradict Saturnina, but she had sliced him open with her gaze.

"Things happen, *vieja*. You don't know."

Saturnina did know. She could see it now. Months before her death, Vania had discovered her living under a tarpaulin in an abandoned courtyard near the city's main cathedral. There Saturnina sat placidly in the corolla of her skirts; next to her a legless man perched on a wide wood plank with furniture coasters for wheels. Shocked and ashamed at the remarkable sight of her mother-in-law in rags, Vania began to visit Saturnina regularly, bringing along scraps of food, bits of soap and clothing, anything Pablo might not notice missing. But on April 1, 1980, Vania never showed up, even though she had promised.

That was a propitious day for Pablo. It was a propitious day for the twelve Cubans who slammed through the gates of the Peruvian Embassy in a minibus. Thousands of Cubans followed them, crossing the threshold of the breached gate, instantly making the decision to give birth to themselves by passing from one life to another, settling on the embassy grounds and rooftops, clinging to trees and fences and drainpipes like nesting bats. In the ensuing chaos, the Cuban government responded, letting every Cuban huddling in the grounds of the Peruvian embassy leave the country, for good measure opening up the prisons and mental asylums and inviting a flotilla of U.S. yachts and fishing boats to take them all away, but not before branding them *Marielitos*, unbearable ingrates, traitors to the Revolution.

Saturnina had assumed the flood of people in the street and the ensuing upheaval had kept her daughter-in-law home. Several weeks later, when Vania still hadn't shown up, Saturnina went to the apartment they had shared and stood on the sidewalk calling up to her daughter-in-law. Pablo shooed her away. When she went again a week later, he hurled a potted geranium at her from the balcony. Angered by his behavior, she went to the police and told them Vania had disappeared at the hands of a husband who regularly beat her.

Standing before Pablo now, the details of Vania's disappearance began to flood Saturnina's mind. The day she showed up at the door with a police officer, Pablo retrieved the note Vania had left him, written in small block letters, unsigned, expressing her disdain for her husband and the communist government. The more agitated Saturnina became in expressing her certainty that something had been done to her daughter-in-law, the more rational

Pablo appeared to the officer, who was himself terrorized by a meddlesome mother-in-law. To the officer, Saturnina appeared unbalanced, filthy, aggressive, and unreasonable. There was something traitorous, still patently bourgeois about the old woman, despite her ragged appearance. The inquiry foundered.

"Why, Pablo?" she asked him now.

Pablo sank to the floor, his lament for the woman he had loved and finally beaten to death sounding like violent hiccups after a bad digestion.

"I want you to leave me alone, *vieja*."

"*Fidel calló*, Pablo. There is someone whose place you can't take who will arrive and redeem us all. He will return."

"Shut up, old woman. I have no religion."

Saturnina put the knife down on the counter and sank to the floor beside Pablo, as he vomited the bile of his life, of the violence he had chosen in fear.

"I never meant to kill her."

Saturnina absorbed his confession into her still resilient flesh, her silent acquiescence rendering for him the magnitude of what he had done. She learned how, when Batista's interrogators were on the verge of killing Tomás, it had been the American, the one who brought the monthly cash payments, who had stood in a darkened corner of the interrogation room, smoking. He ordered the interrogation to stop and then had Tomás released and followed. He assassinated Tomás, recalled Pablo from his exile in New York, and planted Pablo in Tomás's place.

"You killed my son."

"No, Saturnina. I didn't."

"You were part of it."

Saturnina looked into Pablo's eyes as she had looked into the eyes of the American, her son's assassin, when she opened the apartment door and welcomed him into their home as Pablo's guest.

"I never meant to, Saturnina," Pablo sobbed.

Saturnina got up off the kitchen floor. She pitied Pablo He had never been able to replace Tomás, and he had wasted his life drinking in order to forget his betrayal.

"God forgive you, Pablo."

Saturnina left the apartment for the very last time, descending the building's dimly lit stairwell as quickly as her legs allowed.

CHAPTER EIGHTEEN

WHEN HE STOOD before La Milagrosa, Camilo had no prayer to offer. He had no real sense of the wound he bore. Praying was too much like asking, and he didn't want to be beholden, not even to a piece of carved marble, not for anything at all. Amparo would. He could imagine Amparo standing there, asking La Milagrosa to protect him, not to allow him to give up on himself. Amparo would have insisted to Camilo that love endured all, even death, that love had transformed a marble effigy of a mother and child into the eternal Madonna holding the infant Christ. Maybe the solace, the possibility of what Saturnina and Amparo would see in this moment, was better than what he referred to as his realistic despair. If his prayer was never answered, then it would only confirm what he already knew.

Standing on the hood of the Fairlane, Camilo watched the crowd flow past him, tens of thousands of men and women given direction and thrust by his words. Camilo was startled by what was happening around him and what had happened within himself as the words he spoke surged through him—hieratic and lunatic. Whether priest or madman, the yearning for spirit, for something larger than himself, seemed to make itself manifest in him now, not as a political turn away from one thing or another but as a turn toward Love, which was for him now an actual, living presence for the first time in his life. It was his mother and father. It was Saturnina and La Milagrosa, Professor Valle and Amparo. It was the crowd that had surged and ebbed and was now again in flow, a new wave of citizens pushing through, filling the streets.

"*¡Fidel calló!*" the crowd shouted.

"*¡Fidel calló!*" Camilo bellowed.

The crowd roared and swayed, and at some point Camilo either descended from the hood of the *aguacatón* to lead them into the plaza, or the crowd rose to meet him at that height and then drew him along until his feet touched the ground. Camilo linked arms with the person on either side of him. Then they all linked arms and continued walking toward the plaza.

"*¡Fidel calló!*" they shouted.

"*¡Fidel calló!*" Camilo bellowed.

He led the joyful crowd until they could walk no farther. The intersection before them had been rendered impassable, and the moment the approaching crowd saw the blockade, they became fearful and quiet, not knowing what to expect.

"*¡Compañero!*" a man shouted.

Camilo saw the bartender and the men who had followed him, baseball bats and tire irons in hand, standing a few yards away.

"What should we do?" the bartender asked, his grip tight around the baseball bat that rested on his right shoulder.

"What do you want to do?" Camilo said. He could sense the bartender's frustration and the earnestness of his question.

"I want to kill the sons of bitches. I want to see them die for the narrow life they've given me," the bartender said.

The men around him roared their agreement. They shook their weapons in the air, menacing anyone who might step forward.

"I want them to die the way dissidents die—without dignity, without trial," one man shouted.

"Without a word," another man said.

"Without a word," the men all agreed.

"Then we'll have to kill ourselves," Camilo said quietly. "We are those sons of bitches," he added, thinking with sorrow about his own father. "We acquiesced."

"*Compañero,*" the bartender said, "are you telling us not to fight?"

"I'm asking all of you to join us."

"What makes you think we want what you want?" asked one of the men standing behind the bartender.

A terrible hush fell over the crowd as everyone waited to hear what Camilo would say, what he would do.

"We all want the same thing," Camilo said, extending his right hand toward the bartender. "*La revolución es nuestra.* It's ours."

The bartender lowered his bat, and the men behind him lowered their weapons, too. Camilo and the bartender shook hands, and the crowd began to roar and chant. They joined together to move away the looming pile of debris that blocked their path.

Camilo felt as if he were in a dream. Not that he had fallen asleep and was now dreaming, but rather that he was now risen from the still sleeping carapace he used to be. An opaque scrim seemed to lift, and he saw a woman, her figure softly hovering, drifting from point to point before him, veiled like a bride. And behind her, another scrim, the surface of a gossamer *mantilla*, its every intricacy elemental, looming sublime before Camilo.

"I have to see Amparo," he told the woman who was standing beside him.

"You will," she assured him, though she had no idea what he meant exactly.

CHAPTER NINETEEN

Sitting next to Mario on a bench before the martyrs' statue, Pedro Valle tried to inhale the humid late-July air, to push through the constriction in his chest, to move the leaden weights his arms and legs had become. He tried to inhale, but there didn't seem to be any room inside him. He could feel the Spanish patriots tilting headlong and then becoming absorbed into the torrent of hatred and fear unleashed by the governor, swooning like hierophants ecstatic at a blood orgy, their point of confluence the medical amphitheater that had metamorphosed into a kangaroo court. The island's Spanish governor, López Roberts, never imagined that he would lose control of the mob to which he had so officiously pandered. That mob interpreted the governor's detention, not only of the eight medical students but of the entire first- and second-year medical class, a total of forty-five young men, as an affirmation of their collective guilt and an indictment of all expressions of Cuban nationalism.

"I told you," Mario whispered.

He was sitting beside Pedro again, his hands at his sides, clasping the front slat of the park bench.

"Not history, Pedro. A jealous heart. A lot of jealous hearts together."

Pedro watched a gentle smile form on Mario's lips, as if the iron taste of cruelty held some mysterious sweetness in its core. Pedro turned away and looked at the statue again, thinking about the motivations of the men who had destroyed so many lives, and how their cruelty had come to transform itself into a symbol of hope. The day after the colonial governor acted in support of his own interests to detain those forty-five young men, another man, General Crespo, failed to act. It simply wasn't in his self-interest to do so. Crespo had just arrived at his post, and he expected a military parade in his honor. So the day following the detention of the forty-five medical students, ten-thousand armed Spaniards, patriots of the colonial motherland, poured out onto the streets of Havana for this parade, all of them fearful of native Cuban nationalism. Crespo's parade soon became a mob ready to avenge itself with Cuban blood at the desecrated tomb of their General Don Castañón, who grew more beloved to them with each passing hour.

The intricate web that leads us from one thing to another, Pedro thought. That tensile, tender web of coincidences: the tight bud of hatred so deeply rooted in Villaurrutia's heart stretching into full bloom in that cemetery on that January day, triggered by the nervous horseplay of a few young medical students; the governor's tenure drawing to a close, and with it his last chance to reap a windfall both political and monetary; the morally gelatinous Crespo's rise to the position of captain general, Crespo's vanity feeding his insistence on the parade; and that amphitheater transformed into the kangaroo court of a colonial outpost.

"I can imagine it, Mario, as if I had been there."

Indeed, Pedro felt the weight of the image within the cavity that held his heart. To have stood up that day in the amphitheater and argued for the students' innocence, the room bristling with the governor's guards, their damp fingers on the triggers, the mob of armed Spanish soldiers outside, chanting for retribution, already calling out their verdict:

"*¡Mueran los estudiantes!* Death to the students!"

Pedro tried to imagine the barely audible counterpoint of voices dedicated to the expression of the students' innocence. He tried to imagine himself in the role of Juan Manuel Sánchez de Bustamante, the anatomy professor who rose to defend them and managed to save the entire second-year class from execution.

Pedro thought about thrusting his own body from the perimeter to the center of the amphitheater, the words engorging his throat, eloquence dispelling fear. He imagined himself rising from the chair where his interrogators had initially bound him and speaking, his words like a clear cascade of water; imagined his refusal to answer, raising his hands in midair, fingers cupped, waiting, the way he imagined Mario facing his interrogators for that very last time. He could feel the amphitheater's carved mahogany railing and how it would engirth him, separating him from that macabre mass shifting, moving toward its inevitable, deadly resolution.

The first-year medical class of 1871–1872 was defended by Domingo Fernández Cubas, who taught dissection and managed single-handedly to save thirty-seven of the forty-five. Two students were set free. Four spent six months in prison. Twenty were sentenced to four-year terms. Eleven spent six years in the penitentiary. Eight were led to their execution. In 1908 the body of Fernández Cubas was exhumed and laid to rest in the same mausoleum as the eight young martyrs to Cuban nationalism whom he had so valiantly defended.

Of those thirty-seven sentenced to prison by the governor's court, the most noble was Fermin Valdés Dominguez, who, once released, took up the task of vindicating the honor of his eight murdered classmates. By 1873, two years after the event, he had published in Madrid a detailed denunciation of the crime against justice. Fourteen years later, he managed to extract from Don Castañón's son a written statement as to the pristine condition of his father's grave in the days following its alleged desecration. Then he raised the funds necessary to build an enormous mausoleum in Colón Cemetery and successfully petitioned to have the eight bodies of his classmates exhumed. After El Grito de Yara in 1868, Fermin Valdés Dominguez and two other classmates went into the swamps to fight for independence side by side with José Maceo and later Maximo Gómez in the war of 1895.

"They were transformed—from bourgeois dreamers to insurgent nationalists," Mario said. "White and black men, European and African, here on this very ground, joined together in the struggle for independence. Don't tell me it isn't possible, Pedro."

Pedro remembered Mario's words the first time he had visited his studio, which was just a few blocks from the campus, a large attic apartment that Mario had dedicated mostly to his work, relegating a bed and battered armoire to a far corner. Skylights covered nearly half the space, flooding it with light even on an overcast day. He had centered his easel and the small dais directly under the skylights. Pedro recalled the endless tubes of paint and glass jars filled with brushes and spatulas, the viscous clots of paint that formed a pattern on the floor and on the surface of Mario's rustic work table. Stretched canvases leaned against a nearby wall. Rolled canvases and picture books filled every remaining nook. And resting on the easel was a painting of a young woman standing, her dark hair spreading its tendrils along the curves of her body, a standing *maja*, her face left inexplicably unfinished, blank, except for a pendant pearl in each earlobe. He and Mario had been arguing when Mario pulled out a loose bookplate to show him the oil painting by Diego

Guevara depicting the young medical students soon after their execution, their bodies thrown into a common grave somewhere in San Antonio Chiquito.

Sitting on the park bench now, Pedro tried to imagine the moment when each of the eight students understood the leaden finality of his life. He flinched, drawing his shoulders up in what had become an habitual gesture. He could hear the sound of the gunshots, see the rifles recoiling hard into the shoulders of the executioners, feel the young martyrs' bodies slumping back, then forward, their movement constrained by the rope and the pole; he could see their limbs and upturned faces.

He remembered the eagerness with which Mario had shown him the bookplate, as if it were the evidence that proved possible the metamorphosis from dreamer to insurgent. How it was sitting there, tucked inside one of his many books on Goya. In Guevara's painting the bodies seemed to defy gravity. The chaotic tangle of arms and legs Pedro previously imagined heaped before the firing squad had, for Guevara, formed an intricate pattern. In Guevara's painting the bodies seemed to flatten and weave themselves into the air, floating Chagall-like out of the mass grave.

Mario was about to return the Guevara bookplate to its place but started instead to talk about Goya. The pure madness of seeing clearly, Mario said. The torment of understanding, of being able to see through capricious jealousy and ignorance, the violence of willful arrogance. Baudelaire had understood Goya's ability to see the monstrosity of being human; that was why he commented on the Spaniard's ability to suture the real and the fantastic. What Goya had done in *The Second of May* was eschew the fantasy of a single hero. 'This I saw,' Goya kept repeating as he stood in the street in the middle of the pitched battle that was taking place around him, the artist serving as witness to history and so choosing to strip the historical moment of sentiment, of painterly conventions tied inevitably to ideologies, set ways of telling and ignoring what had actually happened. There was no official version of the Napoleonic epic for Goya, Mario insisted. Goya was a Spaniard capturing the heroism of a faceless, collective hero—the Spaniards who stood against the French army and were executed in the street before the barricades on the 2nd of May, 1814, in the War of Independence.

"A faceless, collective hero. That's how I should write about you, Mario. That's the story I should tell—how I betrayed the collective hero."

The words poured from deep within Pedro, sliced

across the decades since Mario's death, since his own improbable release from prison, and emerged as something so obvious he couldn't quite believe it had never occurred to him. He picked up his briefcase on the bench next to him and opened it.

"I can write the truth of what I did." Pedro shaped the words carefully, haltingly, as if he were frightened of breaking a spell that had been cast over him.

The manuscript was before him, its pieces shifting, becoming an actual space through which he was moving, seeing each pillar and curving turn of his argument until he was almost at its end, until what Pedro had been trying to say for decades about Mario, about his betrayal of Mario, formed solidly within the span of his gaze.

Pedro reached out to touch the words floating in midair before him. He could see and feel for the very first time the bridge suspended across the terrible emptiness within him, that space between the man who betrayed his friend and the man who stood contrite, ready to atone for his sin. Sitting on a bench in the Park of the Martyrs, Pedro felt time flowing in both directions. He felt mesmerized, and he worked to absorb and remember every intricate turn of the vision before him. Lifted and succored by the breeze, by the rhythm of the ocean, he felt weightless, potent in the knowledge that he had been chosen to see and know. The weight he had carried for so long on his shoulders began to shift. Then the sound of jangling bells and the sight of a monstrous, gargantuan snail interrupted him, shattering the moment.

CHAPTER TWENTY

It took Pedro several moments to realize that the snail was actually a wiry man pedaling mightily, pulling the canopied, two-seat carapace of a bicycle cab along behind him, steering with one hand, with the other waving. Above the cab's faded red-and-yellow awning flapped a sign that read, "*Justicio's Coche*." The driver seemed to be waving at him, but Pedro was too angry to wave back. He wanted to remain mesmerized. He didn't want a ride to anywhere, and he found it annoying that this Justicio had returned to pester him.

Pedro looked at his watch. It was just past four o'clock. In the afternoon heat, he could feel the weight on his shoulders growing again, the slow distillation of his energies shifting downward, toward the bedrock of his soles and the dusty ground. The sorrow that replaced his vision threatened to overwhelm him once more. Pedro retreated, letting the edges of his mind become entangled with the sound of the waves in the distance and the sun's rays, which beat down on him mercilessly. The anxiety curled upward from his belly to his throat, but he couldn't ignore Justicio, the underfed man who pulled overfed tourists for a pittance, standing only a few yards away astride his bicycle. To Pedro, he looked like a snail ensnared, caught in the harness of a cumbersome shell. Pedro wanted to run, but his legs felt weak, disconnected from his torso. Pedro faltered. He knew that Mario would have drawn a line, laying it down like rail and trestle, between himself and any injustice.

"Jealousy, Pedro."

Pedro squinted into the sun and saw Mario standing in silhouette, the snail man just a few yards behind Mario. In the dreams he had of Mario, Pedro often found himself at the edge of the ocean piecing together the bits and pieces of his friend's flesh, a line of railroad tracks looming behind the sand dunes, a breathing presence that waited for him. The actual rail line, *Ferrocarriles Consolidados de Cuba*, stretched like a membrane of nerves for 2,900 miles over the island, the longest segment running west to east like the spinal cord of an enormous crocodile, from the

ELIZABETH HUERGO

Province of Pinar del Rio to the tip of Oriente. Those freight lines that ran the land's bounty—sugar, coffee, copper, nickel, tobacco—to the ports where it would be dispersed into the world. Land and bounty that rarely fed their own. Passenger lines that served the bigger cities and towns. The system had been built by the British around the turn of the nineteenth century and then left behind, an empire's residue trailing into the next century, its origins obscured by time, disappearing like the lives of the stricken Chinese laborers who built the system piece by piece, with their sweat and blood. Rails and trestles, Pedro mused; trolley tracks, the sort that crisscrossed the city of Havana, carrying workers, shoppers, tourists from point to point throughout the day.

Pedro squinted into the sun, trying to look at Mario and the snail man standing yards behind him, but all he could see were shadows. He remembered stepping onto the trolley on a bright spring day and seeing a beautiful young woman, her hair cut short, her eyes and cheekbones pronounced, the curve of her neck and shoulders, the soft glow of her skin revealing themselves to him as if he had discovered her lying in a just-open shell raised mysteriously from the depths of the ocean. He felt strangely moved by her beauty, frightened by the furtive desire she stirred in him. He felt the impulse to move toward her and say—but there was nothing to say. Language had dropped away, and he had become a pair of unblinking eyes, capable only of gazing at her. Pedro purposefully missed his stop that day. He wanted to see where she lived, where she was going, because surely if she rode this trolley every morning, then he would be there, too, for an eternity if necessary, to watch her pass from one part of the city to another.

The trolley tracks seemed to Pedro infinite, delaying for too long his desire to know where she lived. He tried to calculate whether he could step off the trolley when she did and feign not having seen her, raising a hand to his eyes to block the sun and then squinting, as if to take a closer look and so demonstrate that, no, however beautiful she was, he hadn't noticed her. When the trolley stopped and she rose from her seat, oblivious of Pedro's presence, she smiled and thanked the conductor and stepped off onto the street. Pedro remained paralyzed in his seat, fearful of revealing himself, reduced to straining to see which direction she took as the trolley pulled away.

At the next stop, he got off and began to walk back in the hope that their paths would cross. But he didn't see her again, not until the following summer, though she had been haunting him, though he took the same trolley at the same time every Saturday morning for weeks to follow, hoping he might see her and be able to raise a hand to his eyes and squint and say the words he had so carefully composed in his mind. His hope of ever seeing her again on the trolley began to diminish.

When Pedro arrived at Mario's first faculty exhibit, he searched for his host to thank him, to express his congratulations. He hadn't seen Mario since the luncheon for the American fellow and had been heartened to receive the handwritten invitation to the opening. Mario extended his hands in greeting, but all Pedro could see was the young woman standing next to him, the young woman he had seen in the trolley.

"Where are my manners?" Mario asked, his eyes following the line of Pedro's gaze. "Pedro, I'd like to introduce you to Sonya."

"Did I take her from you, Mario?" Pedro called out plaintively to the dark outline of his friend, who stood before him in the bright sunlight.

"Jealousy, Pedro," Mario repeated.

"You can't take *La Virgensita*," Justicio explained. "She belongs to all of us."

"What?"

"Would you like to hold her?"

"Hold her?"

"It's very comforting. Let me know. You can if you want to," Justicio insisted, his voice revealing his relief.

Pedro took a hard look at the icon, noticing it for the first time. Is that what had happened? At that faculty exhibit, when he finally met Sonya, had Pedro begun to plan his conquest of her? Pedro's thoughts shifted to the memory of the trolley's bell striking, the forward pull of the car after Sonya stepped off and the conductor released the brake and accelerated, causing the passengers to steady themselves; shifted to the web of tracks laid by pickax and shovel, by the brute force of indentured Chinese laborers. Of how those "coolies," as the British called them, had disappeared, become the anonymous amalgamation that had built the tracks that ensured prosperity and then disappeared, with little prosperity of their own, the way Mario had disappeared.

That web of tracks that crisscrossed the city; the same web that in his dreams led him back to Sonya; back to Mario and his constant identification with the human refuse of every epoch, accepting no cruelty or injustice as a given; and back to himself in some terrible moment of acknowledgment that he had taken Sonya from Mario, who had loved her perhaps more and better than Pedro had ever loved her. It occurred to Pedro that when Mario called and asked to meet him in the café for what would be the very last time, he already knew Pedro would betray him, and that of the two men only Pedro had never realized it.

"All of us," Mario had told him that day in the café, "every generation believes its experiences are unlike any other."

Mario had gone on to say something else as well, something about the first lie, the one we tell ourselves, but Pedro couldn't remember anything except the image of an intricate web of nerves that wraps and binds itself to the flesh. It struck him how, toward the end of his life, Mario's paintings began to change drastically, almost as if he knew how much time remained, and how that awareness had accelerated Mario's development. The beautiful, erotic nudes Mario had delineated so minimally with line and color suddenly became morbid, grotesque, as if the sitter had been skinned alive and then matted over in viscous clots of paint that formed cracked webs of pattern and color, the sitter's identity subsumed, merging into the background, which also appeared livid and violent. The European art dealers were mad for the paintings, but Pedro could barely look at them. He couldn't stand the way the paintings' edges seemed to devour their subjects, rendering each body a thing enmeshed, incapable of escape.

"Did I take her from you, Mario?" Pedro called out plaintively to the dark outline of his friend.

Pedro was guilty, but there was nothing he could do now but cover his head with his briefcase as if he were still avoiding the blows the guards had inflicted on him, once and then twice, again and then again for no reason Pedro could grasp, as his eyes fixed on a corner of his half-lit cell where another prisoner had written something, something that began to grow as large as the world in its singularity, in its ability to exclude the truncheons striking him, the sound of his skin splitting, warm blood spilling from his body, ribs snapping like dry twigs underfoot, and like twigs, their ends splintering, pressing sharply against his lungs. Pedro became a pair of eyes, his will concentrated on the single task of reading the words scratched onto the surface of the cell wall, eyes that refused to feel the introduction of some cold, unyielding shard into his body. *History is the lies we agree on*, he remembered reading.

"I knew you had been in that cell before me, Mario. That you'd put those words there for me to find that day."

"I didn't, Pedro."

"You must have."

"Voltaire?" the dark silhouette before him insisted, laughing. "I would have written something original, entirely mine."

"That could have been my penance, you know. You having the last word. It could have been my grace."

But he could no longer see Mario and could barely hear himself think over the roar of the ocean and the trolley bells.

"Don't go! Stay here with me!" Pedro pleaded, squinting into the sun, waving his arms toward the near distance where he had seen the dark outline of Mario's body, the outline of the past, receding.

"I won't leave you," Justicio insisted to the old professor.

CHAPTER TWENTY-ONE

"Saturnina, muerta de hambre (y falta de justicia),
¿Cual es la verdad?
¿Cual la turbación?
Dicen los mas gorditos (traicioneros y tragaderos)
Que lo cuanto que sufrimos es necesidad, nada mas."

Once outside, Saturnina could see that in the time she had spent with Pablo, the street had swelled with ancient Fords and Buicks, motorcycles and bicycles. Tailpipes were spitting plumes of blue smoke. Car horns were blaring. Everyone who wasn't in the street was leaning from a window or a balcony, shouting, calling out to one another, their arms thrust into the afternoon heat.

"*¡Permiso!*" a young boy behind her called out.

Startled, Saturnina stepped aside. The boy was pushing

a grocery cart, the elderly relative seated inside jabbing his walking stick in the air. Behind them came a band of men with trumpets and cymbals, the last one of their group pounding so loudly on his drums that Saturnina had to cover her ears with her hands.

She looked up toward the balcony one last time. There Pablo sat, his hands clasping the iron rails, his swollen, tear-stained face pressed against them. Saturnina looked away, physically turning from the terrible mix of anger and sorrow she felt welling up in her again. She reached inside the bag of tesserae hanging from her waist and touched the plastic box in which she kept the photograph of Tomás. Pablo's confession had left her weak, empty of everything but the fear that she had abandoned Vania and would never be able to explain to Tomás this terrible thing that she had allowed to happen to his wife. Amidst the din of the crowd, Saturnina was aware only of the coiled, overheated knot of her anxiety. Tomás would never forgive her; his return would be delayed again.

She stood on the front steps of the building where the three of them had once lived happily. The crowd appeared to her as an enormous, turbulent river, its waters coiling from one bank of an ancient riverbed to the other. She understood her error now with a clarity that had been absent, and her heart was breaking under the weight of the recognition that she had failed Vania and Tomás both. Against Pablo's perpetual drunkenness, hadn't her obligation toward her daughter-in-law been even greater? The tight coil of anxiety within the old woman shook yes to her terrible question, and Saturnina sobbed. She remembered touching the wound from which the life of her son had poured, the ridged stiffness of his skin, the way death had transformed him into someone other than the son she had known. And then that memory began to commingle with the image Pablo had impressed upon her of Vania dying alone.

Through her tears, Saturnina could see the widening river of celebrants beckoning her. She stepped onto the sidewalk and plunged into the swelling tide, fully believing that it would be her last gesture, this final letting go into the waters of an oblivion she very much desired. She would drown in this river, so much a part of her, and find another way to see her son again, to see Vania again, and ask them both for their forgiveness.

The swelling current, however, did not pull Saturnina under, as she expected. Instead it buoyed her across its surface, dipping and thrusting her body headlong, so that she found herself grasping at loose shirttails and collars and in turn being grasped by hands extended in friendship, muscular forearms lifting and passing her along from point to point. The people around her became bits of flotsam that she could cling to, and she became theirs as they all rose and fell in the enormous swell of humanity that found itself anxiously, gleefully making its way to the plaza that day.

Saturnina didn't see the old colonial mansion until she was disgorged by the crowd onto the curving driveway designed for horse-drawn carriages and flanked by ancient ficus trees. Soon after the Revolution of '59, the mansion, like so many ancestral homes, had been seized and given to rural families newly arrived in the city. These *campesinos* had subdivided the house, strung clotheslines along balconies and interior hallways to mark the boundaries for each family.

Saturnina looked around her. The death she expected hadn't come. Instead, there was the growl of hunger in her belly. She rummaged through her skirts for the apron with the deep pockets. She had no bread. She followed the smell of cigarette smoke, hoping to find someone who would feed her. She passed into the mansion's interior courtyard, where she saw two figures.

"It's okay," one of them called out to Saturnina. "Remember me?"

Saturnina squinted. She could see before her the blond and her sad, fragile companion, who together had brought so much consolation to the *camello*'s passengers.

Conchita was nervously chewing the end of one of her sleeves.

"Do you live here?" Amparo asked.

Saturnina said nothing. She wanted to ask the blond why she, Saturnina, had survived for so many years in the streets and Vania had died in her own home, in what should have been a sanctuary. Here she was, so old and mourning the loss of those so much younger than herself. Saturnina could feel the pull of the terrible dark void she had first known before her son's birth and then again after his death, the feeling that she had been absorbed into some enormous black hole, the husk of her body left behind her.

To Saturnina, these two young women were like the bloodstains that anchored her certainty of Fidel's death, of some consolation, forever deferred, some consolation for the battering life had given her. Perhaps this was the moment of grace that she had wept and prayed for at the feet of La Milagrosa so consistently for so many years.

Conchita and Amparo weren't sure how to interpret the old woman's silence. She seemed confused, mired in dust and filth, and barely able to move inside the dense corolla of her skirts.

"Is this your place?" Amparo repeated.

Saturnina shook her head.

"Are you lost? Did you get off at the wrong stop?" Conchita asked, believing the old woman had become disoriented in the chaos of their exodus from the *camello*.

Saturnina squinted and approached the two young women.

"Vania?" she asked one of them.

"Conchita."

"I'm Amparo. Conchita's my friend."

Saturnina wasn't listening. Her gaze had become fixed on the food that lay near the spot where the women had been sitting.

"Are you hungry?" Amparo asked her.

Saturnina didn't answer but only stepped gently toward Amparo and took the bread roll from her hand. Inside was a sliver of ham. Saturnina accepted it, considering for the first time that this experience on the mansion grounds held a different meaning, deep and unfathomable, but one to which she willingly, even calmly, submitted. She lowered her guard and considered Conchita and Amparo as she ate the sandwich. She watched as, without saying a word, Conchita offered her another sandwich from a brown paper bag.

"Aren't you warm in those long sleeves?" Saturnina asked.

"No," Conchita answered, pulling her arms back behind her.

"People ask me about my skirts." Saturnina shrugged, chewing thoughtfully on the sandwich. "'I carry the most important things with me,' I tell them. 'I never set them down.' That's what I say. What do you say, my little angel? What are you covering up in this heat? I saw you through the bus window suffering, always suffering."

"She cuts herself," Amparo said.

"I've asked you not to tell."

"You really think people can't figure out what you're doing, Concha?"

Saturnina popped the last bit of sandwich in her mouth and ran her right forefinger like a knife over her left forearm.

"Why do you cut yourself?" Saturnina asked.

"Why did you follow Amparo onto the bus?" Conchita responded.

"What are you doing here?" Saturnina insisted, never taking her eyes off Conchita. "Why do you cut yourself?"

"It helps. When I'm anxious."

"It must hurt."

"Not as much as other things," Conchita said.

Saturnina leaned forward and touched Conchita's hands, pulling her gently toward her.

"You don't have to do this."

"How do you know?" Conchita asked her.

Saturnina stood up.

"We must find Camilo."

"Camilo?" Amparo asked.

"We only know one Camilo," Conchita said, glancing at Amparo.

"Why don't you sit for a while? There must be a faucet around here," Amparo said.

"Camilo needs you. You know that better than I do."

"Camilo who?" Amparo called out to Saturnina.

Saturnina was already walking out of the mansion's interior courtyard, leaving them behind.

"Where are you going?" Conchita called out to her.

"To the mouth of the river," Saturnina called back.

Saturnina reached the mansion gate and looked across

the ocean of unfamiliar faces. She caught a glimpse of two of her street children bobbing in the distance. They had seen her first and started to make their way toward her, as if she were a floating log in a rushing stream. Clutching the iron rail of the gate, Saturnina leaned as far as she could into the street, but she couldn't catch them. She watched as the children rode the crest of a human wave, then sank down beyond her sight.

"Wait for us," Amparo called out to her from the mansion's curving driveway.

Saturnina looked back and saw Amparo and Conchita walking quickly toward her. It was too late. Saturnina had already released her grip on the iron rail, rising on the crest of the next wave, catching a glimpse of the children as they waved back and called out her name, then falling into the wave's trough. By the time Saturnina was hoisted up again, the children had disappeared. Saturnina began to weep. This sinking away from sight and suddenly seeing again what was so beloved, this quick alternation between the fear of loss and the glee of something precious found, was too much for an old woman.

The crowd ebbed and flowed. Its rhythm triggered Saturnina's memory of the day in 1959 when she and Vania had along with all their neighbors crowded onto

ELIZABETH HUERGO

the streets of Havana to greet their liberator, Fidel, the one who would free them from the terror of Batista. She remembered, too, the devolution of that joy, the slow transformation of that promise into this tight coil that was finally coming undone before her so many decades later.

Saturnina felt a powerful tug at her waist. Amparo and Conchita were grabbing her skirts and reeling her toward them until they landed together within the deep archway of a building's entrance. From there, the three women watched the confluence of people pushing, laughing, screaming, banging on pots and pans, shouting, chanting, stomping, each person trying to be heard over the others, all of them pushing their way toward the plaza. Amparo took Saturnina by the shoulders and held her, barely able to hear her sobs over the noise around them.

"Let's go up to the roof," Amparo shouted, leading Saturnina and Conchita through the entry and up to the fifth floor.

Eventually they found the door to the roof and pushed as hard as they could against it, but it wouldn't budge.

"What do you want?" someone called out, his voice deep, threatening.

"We want to get away from the crowd," Amparo said. "Please help us."

The door opened abruptly. Amparo, Conchita, and Saturnina found themselves face to face with two men, one armed with a baseball bat, the other, a large man, hunched over, bare-handed, a green cap on his head and a menacing scowl on his face. Behind them, three men huddled together, their backs turned to the door.

"Saturnina?" the man in the green cap asked. "Saturnina, where have you been all this time?"

Saturnina raised her chin and squinted at him, oblivious to how filthy and tattered she appeared, uncertain whether she should tell this stranger all the details of her day.

"Don't you recognize me, Saturnina? It's Armando."

Armando took off his cap. Saturnina, holding on to Conchita's arm, took a step toward him.

"You stood next to him. You saw him die."

Saturnina embraced him.

"After I left Vania and Pablo's, did you stop by?" Saturnina asked, almost coquettishly.

"I did. Pablo told me you didn't live there anymore. 'Cats don't leave forwarding addresses,' he said over the intercom. Then he stopped answering. The bastard. He kicked you out on the street, didn't he? I telephoned every day. Vania came to the phone and told me you had left. When I asked her for your new address, she hung up on me."

"Poor Vania."

"Poor me. You were my lighthouse, Saturnina."

"You couldn't find me?"

"No, but I managed to keep you with me." He smiled, tapping his heart.

"What are they doing?" Conchita asked, pointing a long-sleeved arm toward the other men.

Armando led the three women over to the ham radio, explaining how, hours earlier, when the rumors of Fidel's death could be heard everywhere and the government's silence was deafening, the men had taken the risk of carrying the contraband radio up to the rooftop.

"I thought it was a rumor," Conchita said.

Though Conchita was addressing Amparo, it was Armando who answered: "If it was, it isn't now."

"What will happen to us?" Conchita asked.

No one said anything. The only sound Saturnina could hear against the din of the crowd five stories below was the radio popping and crackling, shuttling its message across that anonymous relay, passing from point to point. On that 26th day of July, the news that Fidel and his brother had fallen traveled rapidly to the towns and villages across the island because of Armando and his fellow dissidents. Their radio began the relay of the day's news from the city of Havana to Camagüey, from Camagüey to Villa Clara, from Villa Clara to Santiago de Cuba, from Santiago de Cuba to Sancti Spiritus, from Sancti Spiritus to Matanzas, and then back again, forming an invisible circuit, like a magic ring that engirthed the island.

"Fidel cayó y Fidel calló," Saturnina said.

Armando, Conchita, and Amparo all looked at Saturnina, but she said nothing more. Instead she rose to her feet and began to make her way toward the rooftop door.

"Where are you going, Saturnina?" Armando asked her.

"To find Camilo."

"Let's go with her, Conchita," Amparo said.

"It can't be your Camilo," Conchita said.

"Of course not, but it's a funny sort of day, isn't it?" Amparo said.

Armando glanced at Conchita and then at the men who had courageously accompanied him up to the roof that day. One of them, headset on, turned and flashed a raised thumb, releasing Armando from any obligation to stay. Armando got up and followed the three women out into the street.

Saturnina stood on the steps of the building, Amparo, Conchita, and Armando beside her. As she prepared to launch into the crowd in search of Camilo, she thought back to the time long ago when she had first known him. She had no more control over her changing body than she had over Camilo, who had looked at the ground and questioned whether that belly of hers had anything to do with him. After she pleaded with him, he turned his back and walked away, and Saturnina remembered going to the edge of the sea that day, wondering what it would be like simply to walk in, deeper and deeper, without any intention of walking out again; to let the saltwater close over her head and the heaviness in her lungs grow until it became like the heaviness in her belly. She had stood at the water's edge for a very long time after Camilo left, waiting for some sign of what to do. Then God spoke firmly in her ear, His words erupting from someplace deep within her, and she left, making her way back home and into her mother's arms.

Thinking of the boy long ago who had fled from her, Saturnina knew she had to explain to him now that he was bearing witness to something that had long been in gestation; something that had exceeded the life span of their son Tomás, and that came close to exceeding her own. There it was all around her, here and now: the coming forth of something as it turned and shifted and prepared itself to be expressed, the first cry already latent in lungs that had not yet contracted, filled for the first time with air. Camilo would need more mettle than he had ever shown her, of that she was certain.

Saturnina noticed Armando watching her.

"It's me, Armando," she said. "I cooked for all of you, encouraged all of you."

"I want to get you home safely before nightfall," he answered her.

"I am home. Don't you know that, boy?"

Saturnina turned away, her gaze absorbed by the turbulent, churning mass of people before her.

"Do you know where she lives?" Armando asked Conchita.

Conchita shook her head.

"I don't think she has a home," Amparo said.

The late-afternoon sun that had shone so brightly on the rooftop was now, at street level, golden, filtering at a slant through the trees and the gaps between buildings.

The scene was different from what Saturnina had expected. The tangle of bodies and sounds was chaotic, fearful—yet somehow organized and soberly focused.

"We must find Camilo," Saturnina told them.

Amparo and Conchita linked arms with Saturnina, and Armando led the way, pushing through the mass of people.

"*¡Fidel calló! ¡Fidel calló!*" the crowd chanted.

"*Fidel cayó y Fidel calló,*" Saturnina shouted back. "My son will return."

To Amparo, Conchita, and Armando, the search for Camilo seemed interminable. Block after city block, they made their way, trying their best to stay together and move with the current of demonstrators. To Saturnina, the search was timeless, the fulfillment of that promise that had been spoken to her as she stood by the water's edge contemplating the end of her life and the life within her, the same promise that she had culled from the death of Tomás.

Saturnina caught sight of the dilapidated building that she called home and its façade of white-and-blue tiles. She looked down at the edges of her skirts, dark and stiff with blood and now dusty from the long day's trek. Then she looked at her companions.

"These streets are mine. I live here. I sleep there," she said, pointing at the building's façade. "But I'm not going there. Camilo's not there."

"What do you want to do?" Armando asked her.

"I want to stay with them," she said, indicating the crowd. "They know where Camilo is. Tomás is guiding them."

"It'd be safer here, *vieja*. Aren't you tired?" Amparo asked her.

Saturnina didn't answer. Instead she plunged into the crowd again, sinking and rising, leaving Amparo, Conchita, and Armando in her wake. Unlike Armando, who had tried to navigate a course toward the plaza,, Saturnina gave no thought to where she might end up. She gave her body to the surging crowd in the same way that she had given her fate to God the night she had jettisoned Pablo and Vania's apartment, the same way she had walked away, pregnant and sorrowful, from the water's edge. The faith she had nurtured daily in something greater than herself, the mysterious hand she felt guiding her every day, now led her to a place just past the capitol.

"Over here," Saturnina called out to Amparo, Armando, and Conchita. She was waving at them, smiling from ear to ear, her tongue peeking through her broken teeth. "Look," she said, pointing up at a second-floor balcony.

Saturnina's companions looked up to see the sky shifting above them, clouds trailing westward toward the far horizon, their billowing surfaces beginning to change in the light of the setting sun. They could see the crowd before them. Everyone seemed to be crying out in one voice, plaintively demanding to be heard.

"Look," Saturnina insisted, pointing again.

"It's Camilo," Amparo said, a look of disbelief on her face.

"You're right," Conchita said.

"Of course I'm right," Saturnina answered.

She was pointing up at the balcony where Camilo stood addressing the crowd.

"They're waking up from a deep sleep," Saturnina said. "Help them, Amparo. Help Camilo. He'll leave without you. And you will always regret it."

"We can't leave you here, Saturnina," Armando said.

"Did you hear that, Tomás?" Saturnina tilted her face up to the sky and smiled. "You are always with me."

"Come with us, Saturnina. Let's go see Camilo together," Armando coaxed her.

"No. I found Camilo. I don't need to speak to him. You

tell him to bear witness to the birth. He was a coward the first time. Tell him he needs to have more guts than he's ever had. Go on. I have something else I have to do."

"Don't go," Conchita said.

Saturnina smiled. She looked at Conchita and saw Vania, Vania's frailty, her lack of an internal compass to guide her.

"Don't take on more pain than belongs to you," Saturnina said, squeezing the girl's hands.

Before any of them could say anything else to her, Saturnina pushed back into the crowd and disappeared.

CHAPTER TWENTY-TWO

★

"COME BACK," Pedro shouted at the dark outline before him.

He heard the brass bells jangling, the sound bringing him back to the present. He opened his eyes, expecting to see Mario, but in Mario's place stood a weather-beaten, muscular old man in a faded tee shirt and dungarees, straddling an ancient Schwinn Spitfire. The old man was staring intently at him as if he expected an answer.

"You okay?"

"I know you."

"Justicio. We met this morning."

"I still don't want a cab," Pedro said, shaking an unsteady hand at him. The words seemed much harsher to Pedro than he intended. "Not today, I mean. Thank you. Justicio."

"Why'd you keep waving and calling out to me?"

"I didn't." Pedro looked down at the ground and shook his head from side to side. "Did Sonya send you? My wife, did she send you?"

"I don't know your wife."

"She did, didn't she?" Pedro insisted. "Go back and tell her I will keep my promise. I know how to finish now. I know what to say. Tell her."

"You look so alone."

"I'm not."

"You look it."

"I'm not."

"I know the feeling. Sometimes I think my wife Irma is riding in the backseat with me all day. When I get home, it's like I never left. If it isn't Irma, it's *La Virgensita* here in her plastic sleeve and bells. Coming or going, there's always some woman steering us around, eh? But I always let them. It's better that way."

"Do you want something?"

"You called me over, remember?"

"I didn't," Pedro insisted.

"You were covering your eyes with one hand and waving at me with the other."

"You've got some euros slipping out of your pocket," Pedro warned him, relieved to change the subject.

"That doesn't happen too often." Justicio grinned sheepishly. "Everything's different today, eh?"

Pedro wasn't sure what he meant, but he was too tired to ask.

Justicio extended his callused right hand toward Pedro. "Let me give you a lift home."

"I don't have any—"

"On the house. I've had a bountiful day. Sad and strange, but bountiful."

Justicio pulled the corners of his mouth down in a deprecating, half-silly way, using both hands to tuck the euros back into his pockets. The bells started to sway and jangle in the breeze again.

"Come on." Justicio gestured toward the bicycle cab.

"I couldn't."

"Remind me. What's your name?"

"Pedro Valle."

"Señor Valle—"

"Professor."

"Professor Valle, you don't look like you weigh a hundred pounds soaking wet. Come on."

Pedro didn't feel like arguing. He was tired, and the wicker cab seemed very comfortable all of a sudden, so he climbed in, gripping with one hand the aluminum bars that supported the faded red-and-yellow canvas awning, with the other holding fast to his briefcase.

"You're going the wrong way. I live on Calle I in El Vedado."

"Too much traffic that way today," Justicio called back over his shoulder as he turned the bike south along El Paseo de Martí, leaving El Parque de los Martires and the statue of Máximó Goméz behind them and, just on the other side of the park, Avenida Céspedes.

Pedro was certain that Justicio, unable to sustain their combined weight, would crash the bicycle. After a few minutes, though, he felt lulled by the breeze on his face, by the rhythm of Justicio pedaling along streets Pedro had not seen in years. He glanced over to his right and found Mario next to him, his head turned at an angle to look back at the Park of the Martyrs, a wistful, melancholy look on his face.

"We never used to come here. Too far off our beaten track."

"We believed martyrdom happened to other people," Mario whispered.

Pedro looked intently at Mario, understanding his friend's sense of irony and how, with the slightest inflection of his voice, Mario was asking him to consider the space they were crossing together in the company of Justicio. Behind them, slowly receding in the distance, was the statue of Máximó Gómez, who joined the rebel army of Carlos Manuel de Céspedes shortly after Céspedes's Grito de Yara on October 10, 1868. History was that intersecting web of streets and avenues, Pedro thought, watching the coordinates rise and fade away in time to the rhythm of Justicio's pedaling, the plastic-bound image of the Virgin swaying from side to side. Pedro could see Céspedes rising before him like a glassy, shimmering plane, then shifting, rolling, intersecting with Gómez, the great warrior, himself rising and intersecting with Martí, poet and legislator. Céspedes and Gómez and Martí: They appeared to Pedro as intersecting lines and planes that he and Mario and Justicio were crossing together in the bicycle cab, the bicycle's wheels seemingly lifting off the ground like an enormous seabird in flight, its feet occasionally skimming the sunlit surface of the water.

Pedro could see Céspedes freeing his slaves, his decision intersecting with the desire of a small group of like-minded plantation owners intent on declaring Cuba's independence from Spanish colonial rule. Céspedes rolled and sank, and Pedro could see Máximo Gómez, who trained that rebel army, drawing on his experience of fighting and winning against the Spaniards on Hispaniola. Pedro looked over Justicio's bent shoulders at El Paseo de Martí, which was shimmering before them. He watched Gómez rolling and sinking away, and Martí rising, in January of 1895, to join Gómez in Santo Domingo and begin the Second War of Cuban Independence.

Céspedes and Gómez and Martí: Maybe it was that simple, Pedro thought. A handful of rebels taking on the Spanish empire, the basic thrust of their political argument, the right of Cuba to be free and democratic, enduring for more than a century after their deaths despite the turmoil fomented internally by competing empires that sought to quell those independence movements, subordinating, harnessing them to their own narrow interests.

"Mario—"

"I'm not Martí."

"I wasn't going to say that. Not exactly."

"I don't like to write. I left that up to you, remember?"

"You died before your time. There was still so much left for you to do."

"Was there?" Mario seemed to be deliberating the possibility carefully.

"You went charging into that fray unprepared."

"There was no way to prepare for the battle we faced. Even for those of us who are avid readers of history."

Pedro watched Mario wink and turn his head. Easy come, easy go, Mario seemed to say. His response confused Pedro. Pedro expected anger—would have understood anger. What he sensed instead was Mario's pacific acceptance, despite the fact that he had left so much undone. Pedro remembered the roll of canvases Sonya had untied and shown him many months after his release from prison. They were Mario's last paintings. She had gone to his studio and taken them shortly after Mario's arrest.

"You stole them after the militia sealed his studio?"

"I preserved my husband's work," she retorted, indicating with the expression on her face that there would be no debate.

"How did you get in?"

"I told the new landlord I was Mario's sister. That I had traveled from a distant province. He let me in. For a fee."

"We shouldn't keep them. It's dangerous."

"This is history, too, Pedro."

Pedro knew better than to argue with her. He sat on the edge of their bed and studied the canvases, how the viscous clots of paint sometimes metamorphosed into lines, words, shapes made from scrawled words. All they evoked for Pedro was the weight and certainty of Mario's death—and fear, mortal fear.

"Put them away, Sonya."

"You're jealous of a dead man."

"They should have killed me instead."

Through his tears, the canvases appeared to Pedro as a palimpsest of handwritten letters, one layer of language over another and another, messages he could not decipher, missives crossing toward him from the land of the dead and in a language he could not speak. Sonya lifted the edges of another canvas where Mario had started to depict his favorite *maja*, only this time she was standing before an executioner, his rifle raised. On the back of the canvas, in Mario's handwriting, appeared the words "The Execution of the Virgin."

"Is that the title?" Pedro asked Sonya.

"I don't know."

"This is his last love letter to you."

"Why would you say that?"

ELIZABETH HUERGO

"You were the model for his *maja*."

"He's not addressing me. He's addressing something as large as life."

"You were life to him."

"Just look, Pedro."

"What else do I do?"

"Don't worry, Professor. I'm a professional. Never take my eyes off the road."

"What?" Pedro called out above the whir of the bicycle's wheels against the pavement.

Justicio turned around, still pedaling at full speed.

"Professional. Never take my eyes off the road," he insisted, pointing with the forefinger of his right hand to his eyes and grinning broadly. "Don't worry."

Pedro smiled back nervously. He hadn't heard a word. All he wanted was to see Sonya and confess to her his betrayal of her husband. He thought about Mario's unfinished canvases. He thought about Martí's last letter, also unfinished. 'We will close that path with our blood,' he had written, referring to the looming Goliath of northern annexation, the U.S. Then he died hours later. He mounted his horse and led his men into the fray at the Battle of Dos Rios, believing it was his duty to fight for the independence of Cuba. Perhaps what Mario shared with men like Martí and Gómez and Céspedes was their idealism, and maybe that degree of idealism changes a man.

"Politics kills all idealists," he had warned Mario the very last time he had seen him in the café.

"It was jealousy that killed Martí, not politics," Mario shot back, trying not to raise his voice and draw the attention of the girl behind the cash register and the patrons at the tables nearby.

"He led the charge at the Battle of Dos Rios despite his temperament and lack of training," Pedro said.

"It was jealousy that killed him, not a poet's temperament or a lack of training. The other guerrilla generals were jealous of him, of the charisma and intelligence that flowed naturally from him. You were jealous, too, Pedro."

"When was that?"

"Every time running became your most expedient choice. It was never really about history or politics between us."

Sitting in the back of Justicio's bicycle cab, Pedro turned to look at his friend, the uncanny sensation that time had stopped nearly overwhelming him. It was as if Mario and he were both university professors again, and so much of the cataclysmic history that would eventually roil between them like some great river in flood had never happened. In a moment this nightmare would be over, Pedro thought. He would wake up. He would have his youth again. The sensation was so real that Pedro was reluctant to speak and so perhaps interrupt his ability to surface from the nightmare and into full consciousness.

"It was always about Sonya. She was the territory we battled over," Mario whispered, his green eyes blinking thoughtfully at Pedro.

"She loved you, Mario."

"She did."

"She only married me out of a sense of practicality."

"She married you. She cooked your dinners. She woke up next to you. She waited for you all the years you were in prison."

"She was waiting for you, Mario. I was the lousy consolation prize."

"You okay back there, Professor?"

"What?"

"You all right?"

"I've been wrong all along."

Justicio was torn between laughter and pity as he turned to see the funny old professor seated there, his eyes as wide as saucers, his lips trembling as if he had just seen a ghost.

"About what, Professor?"

"Everything, Mario."

"How could you be wrong about everything, Professor?" Justicio asked.

Pedro looked into Justicio's face and gleaned his sorrow. For all his cheerfulness, Justicio seemed preoccupied, enervated. Justicio was letting the bicycle coast between the capitol and El Parque de la Fraternidad Americana. The Avenida Simón Bolívar stretched east before them. Farther on it would become Avenida Salvador Allende and eventually Zapata, leading in a nearly straight line toward El Vedado, La Plaza de la Revolución just to the south.

"The tyranny of time," Pedro said, squeezing his eyelids tightly to keep himself from crying. "Isn't that what you said, Mario?"

"The tyranny of politics that leeches sustenance from a child's bones. That's what I said."

Once again Pedro could feel Mario's words striking him across the chest. He paused to catch his breath, which was coming with difficulty.

Alarmed at the audible discomfort of his passenger, Justicio stopped.

"I can't bear any more trouble today, Professor. Not today," he insisted.

"I'm all right," Pedro said. "I just need to go home."

Justicio looked dubiously at Pedro and then at the image of the Virgin in her plastic sleeve.

"*¡Metí la pata!*" he muttered under his breath. "I stuck my foot in it!"

"Why would you say that, Justicio?"

"No one has ever had any problem in my cab." Justicio was nearly pleading.

"I should go home," Pedro repeated, looking past him, trying not to think of Sonya waiting for Mario and receiving the wrong man instead.

Justicio turned his attention away from Pedro and started to pedal with renewed intensity. The clouds that had lingered in the sky all day were gathering now in the west, pushed by the same wind that Pedro had felt at his back earlier. Twilight was approaching. Seated in the wicker cab, Pedro Valle looked at his wristwatch, but it had stopped just after five o'clock.

"Mario, what will I say to Sonya? She'll know that the university was closed. How will I explain to her that I've frittered the time away?"

How could he ever explain to her the difficulty of facing his betrayal of Mario, of Mario's idealism, his desire for a very different political reality? How could he justify his jealousy? Pedro had let Sonya imagine his detention, and eventually she stopped asking him about it. He watched as, over time, she filled in the spaces of his silence. She explained to him that, when he seemed barely able to recognize her, when he carried on animated conversations with himself or shrank in fear at a distant sound, she simply told herself it was better than what had happened to her first husband, Mario.

"Mario, what will I tell Sonya?"

Pedro saw the tears in Mario's great, blinking cat eyes, and found himself wondering if Mario had looked at his interrogators that way the day they killed him.

"Mario, what was it like? At the very end."

"It was like the beginning."

"That's not an answer."

"It's always the same story, Pedro. The details vary. Your memory shuffles them around. It's always once upon a time, and just the way it happens in a fairy tale, someone decides to take a chance, to be tested, transformed."

"What if he dies trying?"

"That's a transformation, too, isn't it? The trouble with you, Pedro, is that you want the line between history and story to be absolute, but they're really two sides of the same coin. You've been trying to write a scholarly treatise, a definitive biography, an exhaustive confession. I asked you to write a story of betrayal and possibility, but you can never see past the betrayal. That's what's in your heart."

Pedro's eyes opened wide in distress.

"A betrayal of ourselves, Pedro. Remember what Martí said: 'I have lived inside the monster and know its entrails.' If that isn't a poet's, a storyteller's recognition that his life is a quest, that he stands before a force greater than himself, I don't know what is. After Martí's death, the rebels he had gathered together won the Second War of Independence. They defeated Spain. They defeated an empire, Pedro. Then they betrayed themselves. They won, but they acquiesced to the U.S. occupation of Cuba from 1899 to 1902. To get the U.S. troops out, the rebels gave away their sovereignty. They gave in and agreed to add the Platt Amendment to the Cuban constitution, the constitution that Martí himself had penned. They gave away their victory. Now the U.S. could intervene whenever it wanted in Cuban national affairs, which is precisely what the U.S. did for the next thirty-two years. Martí would never have agreed to that. He knew firsthand what it meant to live 'in the belly of the monster.' He would have negotiated very differently."

Pedro knew the truth of Mario's words. He knew how

easy they were to forget. The greed and corruption Mario described was what had opened the way for Batista, whose own corruption and repression opened the way for Fidel. Each event appeared in his mind's eye suspended on an invisible web, vibrating imperceptibly, each moment entraining succeeding moments, until the organs within his own body seemed to quiver and shake. Pedro looked over. He could see Mario in profile, his eyes locked on the horizon.

"You chose," Pedro said, forming the words carefully, part statement, part question.

"There is no history written of those who quietly endure, Pedro. You don't need to travel north like Martí to live in the monster. There are monsters everywhere. They represent some necessary confrontation with ourselves. Their chaos, inflicted upon us, renders us to ourselves, reminding us of something integral that we need to remember."

"What we do, we do to ourselves?"

"What we do, we do to ourselves, Pedro."

CHAPTER TWENTY-THREE

JUSTICIO PEDALED faster and faster, driven by the fear that something was happening to his elderly passenger and the memory of having closed the stiffening eyelids of Fidel and Rafael Pérez just that morning. The memory of that touch and the memories he had of his own sons playing ball in the street with the two brothers commingled with his fears for the delusional old professor sitting in his cab.

"*Virgensita alludame. Virgensita alludame.*"

His repeated plea to the Virgin for help eventually took on the rhythm of his pedaling, the rhythm of the Virgin's image swaying in time to the movement of his body and the jangling bells as he pushed as hard as he could against the pedals. He could hear Pedro in the wicker seat behind him talking to himself, weeping and pleading.

"How can I help you, Professor?"

Justicio wanted nothing more in the world than to console his passenger. He was trembling, and his mind was consumed by the fear that this lucky unlucky day would end for him as it had begun, with the same irreparable loss, some moment he could never undo.

"Only Mario can help me finish," Pedro wailed.

"Is he your son?"

"He's been a brother."

"Where is your brother Mario?"

"He won't help me."

"Of course he will," Justicio insisted. "That's what family's for, Professor."

"How to see, what to do. It's all my choice."

Exhausted by the old man's despair, Justicio turned his attention again to the road, finding himself at the very edge of an enormous crowd that was moving toward La Plaza de la Revolución, blocking his ability to get the ailing professor home. Justicio stopped and looked around him. Every possible side street was blocked with people of every age, each one shouting louder than the others.

The din was deafening; the sight disorienting. Justicio just couldn't understand what anyone was saying or doing. He could see that backtracking along the route he had taken was as impossible as moving forward. The crowd seemed to be swallowing the bicycle cab whole. He sensed Pedro shifting his weight. He glanced back and saw the professor leaning forward in the wicker seat and squinting into the distance.

"Mario?"

"You see your brother?" Justicio asked.

Justicio looked into the distance, following the line of Pedro's pointing finger, and saw an unkempt young man in a short-sleeved shirt standing on a second-floor balcony addressing the crowd, several other speakers behind him. Justicio couldn't make out what the young man was saying. He turned to ask the men and women standing next to him in the crowd, but an odd mixture of glee and fear made them incoherent. No one seemed capable of saying anything Justicio could understand. He could hear chanting in the distance. He watched and heard as the chant curled like a wave and flowed from the center of the undulating crowd outward, but it took him a long time to make out the words:

"¡Fidel calló! ¡Fidel calló!"

Confused, he wondered how the deaths of Fidel and Rafael Pérez that morning could have galvanized such a response. Their families, their friends and neighbors had all grown to love the two misfit brothers, but how was it all these people knew them and came to mourn them? Justicio felt guilty; of course the brothers had touched many people's lives. Who was he to judge? Then another thought crossed his mind, which he tried hard to push away. He glanced at the image of the Virgin.

"*¿Fidel calló?*" he asked her, his eyes wide.

In an instant, the terrible symmetry of the day revealed itself to Justicio: the coincidental deaths of two Fidels, two sets of close-knit brothers. He began to push his way through the crowd using the front wheel of his bicycle to cleave a path, all the while trying to assure Pedro that everything would be all right.

"Mario!" Pedro suddenly called out, leaning forward in his seat.

It was in vain. No one could hear Pedro Valle over the din. The old man shrank into the shell of the cab again and looked around him. He appeared afraid of the crowd, certain that at any moment it would turn around and avenge itself on him personally.

"Don't leave me here alone," Pedro pleaded.

"I'm not going to leave you," Justicio assured him. "Is that your brother Mario? He seems a bit young. To be your brother, I mean."

Justicio could see that his passenger was hyperventilating. The more he looked out into the distance, the more upset he seemed to become, but there was nothing Justicio could say to draw the professor's attention from whatever was agitating him.

"Why have they put me in this cell again, Mario?"

"Take it easy, Professor. The seat's not that small. I'll get you home. We just need to get through this crowd, that's all," Justicio said. "Take a breath. Inhale slowly. Exhale. Slow down."

Justicio could sense that Pedro was receding, pulling into himself like a startled turtle.

"Where are you now, Mario? Please let me hear the sound of your voice."

"I'm right here, Pedro."

"This dirt bunker is so ghastly. Will they ever release me? Will I ever find you?"

Pedro could sense Mario smiling at him.

"I'm here, Professor."

"Mario."

"Justicio."

"I shouldn't have disagreed."

"Why not?"

"I shouldn't have."

"Sometimes we disagree. We can still be brothers." Justicio shrugged.

"Mario, what was it like? At the very end, I mean."

"It's not the end of anything," Justicio said emphatically, wanting to ward off any more bad luck.

Pedro, however, was unaware of anything Justicio was saying or doing. He had shut his eyes tightly in order to escape, retreating from one fear and into another until he found himself lying in his own feces in the damp, narrow grave of the bunker. Then the darkness began to shift. A ghostly light rose, revealing patterns, patches of muted colors, lines and shapes that shifted and turned, emerging, his fears becoming the faces of howling demons and witches that lurched mercilessly toward him until he felt himself slipping along the edge of madness.

"I showed you the photographs," Mario whispered. "Don't you remember? Look, Pedro."

Mario was pointing at the enormous open book on the broad wooden table in his studio. He was dressed in a white, intricately embroidered *guayabera*. Pedro wearing his prison uniform, the fabric stiff with blood and excrement. He smelled like an open sewer. He looked down, ashamed, and peered into the book as if he were leaning over the edge of a precipice. He could see the photographs of Goya's murals, the ones Goya painted on the walls of La Quinta del Sordo, where he lived.

"His deafness intensified his ability to see," Pedro said.

"Did I say that?" Mario smiled.

"You said he became a medium who could see the air filled with spirits, who could see the brutality and the banality in every heart."

"Sometimes, Pedro, he could see goodness, heroism. He'd depict it without sentiment."

"You're calling me sentimental?"

"You have a sentimental attachment to fear, my friend. Close your ears, Pedro. Look."

Pedro was too afraid. The stench of his own body made him want to vomit. He squeezed his eyes shut. His body lurched from side to side as he lay in the National Institute of Agrarian Reform van. Someone gripped him, forcefully hoisted his tense body up and out as if he were weightless, and then set him down again. He could smell the damp earth. He waited for someone to start kicking him. He waited for the blessing of losing consciousness. Instead he felt his back pressed against some rough surface.

"Look."

"I can't. Please don't make me. Everything became entangled in my heart: Batista, Fidel, the Raid, and you, Mario. Everything became one long, inextricable chain of causes and effects. That single revolution, that turn in consciousness that was the Moncada Raid, became for me the point of confluence for all Cuban history, for the events that composed my life, and the lives of everyone I've ever loved."

Pedro remembered how, watching the Raid unfold, Mario had understood, while Pedro, like so many other experts, had failed to see the Raid's import, the several dozen rebels lying dead on the ground, the arrest of Fidel and his brother Raúl and the other men who had remained standing with them. Pedro, like so many others, had concluded incorrectly that the day's battle was a clear victory for Batista, who immediately threw Fidel in prison. At his secret trial a few months later, Fidel spoke eloquently in his own defense, vowing that history would absolve him and giving voice to this idea of absolution that would come to form the cornerstone of the Revolution of '59. The rebellion, the trial, the words Fidel spoke in his own defense—all of it seeped through the public consciousness, coalesced, flowed again, uncontainable, until by May of 1955, popular support for the rebels who had assaulted the barracks and challenged Batista's authority was so great, their hagiographies so often rehearsed, that Batista had to release them, all of them, including Fidel, who found exile in Mexico, where the next phase of the revolution began.

"You were prescient, Mario."

Mario shook his head. "I was willing to look. To see."

"What has absolution meant to Fidel, a Catholic educated in Cuba's finest Jesuit schools and a communist who criminalized religious worship? The penance hasn't been Fidel's. Fidel has grown to a fine old age: well fed, well tended, able still to act in the world, even in retirement, even if only by proxy."

"Have you absolved yourself, Pedro?"

"How could I ask for absolution?"

"We're all sinners."

Whoever had spoken, Pedro knew it was not Mario. This man's voice was sarcastic and submissive. Pedro felt his body flung through space, his head dropped heavily against a rough surface, his face turned to the damp ground.

"It's time," Pedro said.

"Time? Oh, it's almost six o'clock," Justicio said, dropping to the ground, spent from the exertion of carrying his passenger to the shade of a nearby tree.

CHAPTER TWENTY-FOUR

THEIR ARMS LINKED together, Camilo and his companions filled the width of every street as they walked from the blockaded intersection toward a building near the capitol. The din of the crowd was deafening. People were chanting slogans, banging pots and pans, drums and cymbals. They were dancing and praying, their faces gleeful and weeping. Camilo and several others went up to the second-floor balcony to address the crowd before starting off on the final push toward the plaza. As he was speaking, Camilo could see a bicycle cab with a faded awning obtruding along the far edge of the crowd. He found himself distracted by the vehicle, by the manner in which the mass of human bodies in the street seemed to swallow it whole and then spit it out again.

"We've failed," Camilo told the crowd. "We've lacked

the courage to see ourselves, our frailties and our collective strength."

As Camilo spoke, he kept the bicycle cab in his peripheral vision. He saw a thin man pushing the cab through the crowd. He saw the man stop, then make his way in a different direction, toward a slight elevation, a copse of pine trees, the crowd resisting, parting, and then coming together again in the bicycle cab's wake.

Camilo's gaze kept being drawn toward whatever was taking place between the driver and his passenger, both of whom looked like bookends, old and undernourished, one struggling to pull the other out of the cab.

"It's impossible to change anything without changing ourselves, our expectations," Camilo shouted to the crowd. "In the past, we've shared our despair in silence. Now let's share our hopes together and out loud."

The crowd roared its approval, and Camilo waved, stepping off the podium and to one side of the balcony. As he stood waiting for the next speaker, Camilo was startled to see another familiar figure in the crowd. It was Saturnina, unmistakable in her ring of bright skirts, weaving in and out of the crowd's edge and followed by three people, two of whom he was certain he knew.

Camilo continued to peer from the side of the balcony. The more he looked, the more certain he became that he was seeing Conchita and Amparo. Camilo watched Saturnina disappear. He could see Amparo clearly. The urge to call her name and ask her forgiveness was irresistible. Camilo leaned as far as possible over the balcony rail.

"*¡Amparo!*" Camilo shouted. "*¡Amparo! ¡Amparo!*"

"*¡Salvaguardia! ¡Salvaguardia!*" someone else shouted.

"*Amparo y salvaguardia,*" the crowd responded.

"*¡Amparo! ¡Amparo! ¡Te amo!*" Camilo called out, one arm around a nearby column as he strained to catch Amparo's attention, leaning forward just a few inches more.

"*Amparo y salvaguardia,*" a large swath of the crowd started chanting.

"*Amo y apoyo es la revolución,*" another group sang.

"*¡Amparo!*" Camilo shouted.

"*¡Salvaguardia, apoyo, amparo! ¡Te amo revolucíon!*"

"*¡Amparo! ¡Te amo!*" Camilo shouted.

"*¡Salvaguardia, apoyo, amparo! ¡Te amo revolucíon!*" the crowd roared in unison.

As Camilo extended his body farther and farther over the rail, he felt the pack of cigarettes in his shirt pocket slip. Without thinking, he reached for the pack and lost his grip on the column. Camilo found himself tumbling over the balcony's edge, his arms flailing, his hands helplessly clutching the air. The duration of his fall felt like an eternity. He thought about his life and his newfound purpose; he thought about everyone he loved.

"He's fallen," Amparo screamed, fainting to the ground. Armando struggled to catch her before she struck her head.

Instead of hitting the hard ground, Camilo fell on the crowd. Their strong arms and shoulders broke his fall. Then the crowd lifted him up, passing him across from point to point, finally placing him on the ground to rest. Camilo looked up to see the ring of well-wishers gathered around him, smiling, and the clear blue sky, and the sheen of rose-colored light that always presaged the fall and rise of the sun. Camilo was helped to his feet, the dust brushed off his clothes. Shaken and out of breath, once he got his bearings, he realized Amparo was on the far side of the point where he now found himself. He wanted to find her, to tell her everything had changed. He had changed. He could speak now. He could see and say what he wanted and why, and he wanted her.

Finding himself close to the copse of pine trees where he had seen the man push the bicycle cab and its passenger,

Camilo made his way there, hoping the rise of the ground would help him spot Amparo.

On the other edge of the crowd, Amparo had regained consciousness.

"Where is he?" she asked her companions. "I have to see Camilo."

CHAPTER TWENTY-FIVE

PEDRO STRUGGLED to do exactly as Mario asked. He pressed his hands tightly over his ears and tried to summon the courage to open his eyes and bear witness. When he finally dared to look, he found himself at the base of an old pine tree.

"Mario?"

"Justicio. The crowd's too much for you, eh? I don't blame you. They're too much for me."

From the slight elevation where the small copse of pine trees grew, Pedro watched the enormous crowd making its way toward the plaza. He tried to sit up, using the trunk of a pine tree to brace himself. Tilting his head up, he noticed the branches far above him, the stark green needles and the soft blue sky. He could see Mario, too, his green cat eyes blinking slowly at him.

"I'm right here with you, Pedro."

"I must get home, Mario."

"You will."

"Where is Sonya?"

Pedro felt the pressure rising within his chest wall again. He gazed up toward the branches, then extended his right arm out as if to touch Sonya's face. The pain in his chest ebbed, but he was left breathless, frail. He wanted to move, to make his way back to Sonya, but he couldn't. His legs refused his command.

"Can you help me home, Mario? I can't move."

"I'll help you, Professor."

Justicio cradled Pedro in his arms. Then he took the old man's briefcase and placed it under his head.

"Thank you, Mario."

"Yes, Professor. Don't mention it."

Justicio sat on the ground next to Pedro Valle, resigned to the idea that there was nothing else he could do to help him until the streets cleared.

"What do you teach, Professor?"

"You know I teach history."

"What sort?" Justicio persisted.

"The sort no one wants to remember."

"I remember plenty. Lived through even more." Justicio grinned.

Pedro opened his eyes and saw the gaunt cabbie sitting beside him under the pine trees.

"Tell me a story," Justicio insisted, wanting to distract his passenger for as long as possible. "You must know so many. Tell me a story that would make sense of this day."

"There was a very brave man once, a university teacher, who never liked Batista or Fidel. Some of his students protested at the Presidential Palace. Others seized the radio station on the same day and announced over the airwaves their own revolution. They were arrested and killed. The teacher was disappeared."

Justicio looked at Pedro Valle with pity. He could see the old man's face was streaked with tears.

"So many stories. Did you have to tell me a sad one, Professor?"

"Is there any other sort of story? The teacher never foresaw how his words, his desire for political process, could be used to destroy—himself, others. They were so young, and they gave up their lives for a principle."

Justicio wasn't sure how to respond. He only wanted to keep the old man as calm as possible.

"Sometimes, Mario, in my dreams, I succeed in changing your mind. My eloquence keeps you alive. I make you see why you can't enter that fray. Why what was happening would continue to happen in an endless, unmitigated cycle. Why it wasn't worth your life. Why it wasn't worth your students' lives. In my dreams, I can always find you and piece you together. I can undo what I did to you."

Pedro flinched at the wave of pain that coiled through his chest and down his left arm.

"What was the point? The violence that ended your life and theirs—what was the point?"

"The suffering is a mystery, Professor. That's why I pray to *La Virgensita*. She's mysterious. She jangles those brass bells at me. She warns me away from danger. She tells me things I don't understand."

Justicio was relieved to see someone approaching, someone who might help him distract the old professor or get him home.

"Are you Mario?" Justicio asked.

"I'm Camilo. Who are you?"

"Justicio. I was trying to help him," Justicio said, gesturing at the man stretched out next to him under the tree.

"Can you hear me, Professor Valle?" Camilo asked, kneeling beside the old man.

"You look very different, Mario."

"Who's Mario?" Justicio asked Camilo.

"We need to get him to a hospital. Is the bike broken?" Camilo asked.

"How do I come to rest here?" Pedro asked.

"It's fine," Justicio explained. "I just couldn't get it through the crowd."

"Perhaps the same way you came to rest here. In the solace of the landscape, for I can find no better solace now than to think of your ashes, Mario, in this very ground that is also my soul."

"We need to get help," Camilo said.

"That's what I was trying to do. I wanted to help him. This way around the city was supposed to be easier. I've made so much money today. I asked *La Virgensita*, 'Which way should I go?' Whatever *La Virgensita* told me, I got it all wrong."

Camilo turned his attention to Pedro Valle.

"Professor Valle, can you hear me?"

"You told me not to, Mario. You told me to look. I did. I did as you asked."

"Good, I'm glad you did," Camilo said. "Can you move, Professor Valle?"

"You said it was greed. The greed that made the

conquistadores so effective was also their undoing. You said the duplicity that made Batista so useful to the U.S. weakened him and gave rise to Fidel. You said it. I see it now."

"I know you do, Professor," Camilo said. "He's too weak to move, Justicio. Can you stay with him while I go find some help?"

"No, I can't. I can't bear to see another man die today."

"Who did you see die today?" Camilo asked.

"The two brothers I loved as my own. I saw them fall this morning. I closed their eyes with these hands."

Camilo watched as Justicio, kneeling on the ground opposite him, gazed at his hands as if they belonged to someone else. Camilo thought of Saturnina. Here was another witness confirming the truth of Saturnina's words. Fidel and his brother had died. He looked at Pedro Valle. The sight of his old professor, fragile and vulnerable, nearly moved him to tears. Camilo wanted to lead the crowd. He wanted to find Amparo. He wanted to stay with Professor Valle.

"You're a cabbie, Justicio. You must know where the nearest clinic is?"

Justicio nodded. He turned to Pedro and placed a hand over the old professor's heart. "*La Virgensita* is with you. Don't forget. She's mysterious, but she never leaves you."

"Are you leaving me, Mario?"

"I'll get there faster on foot," Justicio told Camilo. "Can you look after the cab for me? That's all I have. My family, *La Virgensita*, and that cab."

"Of course," Camilo answered.

Justicio reached over, took the plastic sleeve with the Virgin's image inside and the string of brass bells, and hung them around his neck.

"I'll be back as soon as I can," he told Camilo, then started pushing through the crowd as quickly as he could.

"Are you leaving me, Mario?"

Pedro struggled to raise himself off the ground.

"Of course not. I'm here," Camilo said, trying to comfort him.

"I should be writing. I'm not even close to finishing. I've made a tangle of the story instead of respecting its simplicity."

Pedro closed his eyes again, searching for Mario in the dark of the prison cell. He could see his friend's green eyes blinking, glowing softly in the dark.

"I failed you, Mario."

"You carried me out of that prison."

Pedro looked at Mario in disbelief.

"You carried me into the light of day. You remembered me. You took me with you to the podium of all those classrooms."

"I didn't have the courage to go with you when you asked. Under interrogation, I spoke your name. I married your wife. I've never atoned. Are you still there, Mario?"

"I'm right here," Camilo assured him.

"I can't see you very well."

"I'm here, Professor," Camilo repeated.

"Where's my briefcase?"

"It's under your head."

"Where is it, Mario? The briefcase. Do you have it?"

"It's here, Professor. Under your head."

"Take it. I want you to see that I tried. I want you to understand that I understand. We betray our own for all the wrong reasons."

"Look at the sky," Mario whispered. "You can see the sky, can't you? The way the day gathers its skirts and draws far away, into the darkness."

Pedro looked and saw the darkening web of the pine branches above him and the skin of the sky, like a cloud crocodile made of coral squares ridged in blue and purple. He tried to pull his body up off the ground. His eyes grew wide, startled as another wave of pain began to surge through his body, striking him, dragging him down and across a jagged surface until he was gasping for breath. When the wave subsided, Pedro felt his strength return.

"I'm going to finish it when I get home."

"I know you will," Camilo assured him. "Justicio will be back soon. Tell me what you did today."

"Today? You know that as well as I do, Mario."

"Tell me anyway, Professor."

"On this day in 1953, Fidel and his men attacked the Moncada Army Barracks in Santiago de Cuba. Afterward, Batista threw Fidel and his brother Raúl in jail for two years. Their incarceration fueled the July 26 Movement and so much social unrest that Batista had to release them."

Pedro gazed up at the birds that had come to roost in the pine branches. Mario seemed to hover over him, somewhere in the distant branches.

"Look at me, Professor Valle. Can you hear me?"

Pedro opened his eyes wide and looked at Camilo's face, but all he could see was Mario hovering over him.

"Of course I can hear you. In '57 Batista's police shot and killed Frank País, one of the leaders of the July 26 Movement. Tens of thousands of people swarmed into the streets to join his funeral procession. There were massive strikes taking place across three of the eastern provinces. Earl Smith, the new U.S. ambassador, arrived just in time to see Batista's goons beat the women standing along the funeral route, just in time to watch Batista bombing his own people, torturing and killing anyone who dissented. It didn't matter how many Cubans wanted Eisenhower to stop sending arms to Batista. Eisenhower insisted he was neutral, all the while providing arms and training to Batista's military. He insisted he was neutral, then had Carlos Prío Socarrás, the legitimately elected former president, the man Batista overthrew, indicted for violating U.S. neutrality laws. To lie that way, to violate our sovereignty—that was what you always wanted me to see and to bear witness."

Camilo was sitting on the ground holding Pedro Valle. The voice that had sounded their history had been reduced to a shallow echo. Camilo felt himself alone before the terrible river whose navigation old Valle had taught him, the way a father teaches his son.

"Even in '58," Pedro continued, "Smith believed it was possible to prop up Batista and conduct a free election. When Batista's candidate, Andrés Rivero Agüero, won the election, Eisenhower sent a secret emissary to persuade Batista to step aside. Eisenhower offered Batista exile in Florida if he would let the U.S. set up a junta that would govern Cuba. I suppose only some people are allowed to be righteous hypocrites."

"If they have enough wealth." Mario smiled.

"If they have enough wealth," Pedro repeated. "Will you ever forgive me, Mario? Have I even earned the right to ask you?"

"Have you forgiven your jailers, Pedro?"

"No. I can't."

"I always forgave you, Pedro."

"That can't be possible, Mario."

"Anything's possible, Professor Valle," Camilo insisted. "Can you hear me? I need you to stay awake. Justicio will be here soon."

"Camilo, is that you? Camilo, are you all right?"

Startled by the familiar sound of Amparo's voice, Camilo turned to see her approaching with Conchita and a man he didn't recognize.

"Amparo. It's Professor Valle. He's having trouble breathing," Camilo called out to them.

"Your professor?" Amparo knelt on the ground across from Camilo.

"What are you doing here, Amparo?"

"We heard your speech."

"We saw you fall over the balcony," Conchita added.

"Do you need help moving him?" Armando asked.

"I'm afraid to move him. He's so weak. I sent someone for help," Camilo explained.

"You're right, Mario. I was afraid to move. I didn't want to see or use what I knew to bear witness. Not the way you did. In '59, Fidel went on an unofficial visit to the U.S. and met Richard Nixon. Nixon asked him about the difference between democracy and dictatorship, and Fidel told him, 'Dictatorships are a shameful blot on America.' He talked to Nixon the way you would to an amnesiac—or an undergraduate."

Pedro laughed. A wave of pain followed, surging through Pedro's body, striking him, dragging him down along a dark, rocky floor.

"Fidel pointed out to Nixon that democracy could not coexist with hunger, unemployment, or racism. During my detention, I came to hate Fidel, but I could also appreciate his intelligence, his refusal to genuflect."

Pedro felt the slow tide of pain building again.

"The briefcase, Mario."

"It's right here. Don't worry," Camilo said.

"The story is yours. The cowardice was mine. You were prescient, saw what I refused to see. It's yours."

"Mine, Professor?"

Pedro Valle could no longer hear the commotion around him, though he could see the darkening web of the pine branches and the crocodile skin of the sky, cloud-echo of the island. He could see the enormous book of maps in his mother's lap and her fingers guiding his, tracing the curving crocodile shape of the island, the long, dark tendrils of her hair forming a canopy around and above him. The coral squares of cloud were ridged in blue and purple; then the breeze and the imperceptible turning of the earth began to pull the squares across the sky, mottled skin expanding: squares into rectangles, rectangles into long streams of color that began to lie down serenely on the horizon in anticipation of the coming darkness.

The blue of the Madonna, the blue of a Venetian sky, of cerulean ink on a snow-white page, the soft wales of veins that had risen over time on Sonya's hands: The breeze quickened, and the colors began to stream across the sky. His mother, pulling his hand gently across the surface of the island's map one last time, conveyed to him silently, eternally, his sense of place. He understood anew:

This earth and sky, and this island in between, placed here, had always belonged to him in the purest sense.

Pedro Valle felt the pressure of the black birds' wings long before the cross-shaped bodies, helixes of dark angels, began to turn and soar in synchrony overhead. The pressure of so many thousands of wings pumping, in unison rising, each body invisibly calibrated to the other. No one had told them; yet within the chambers of their hearts they had known with the precision of a metronome the exact moment to lift their breasts to the sky, to push their bodies into the cloud-ocean, to find their way home in the dusk to the pine trees, the black branches that bristled and welcomed. They knew in the blood; in the time that exists only in the blood.

Pedro Valle could see his mother's fingers in silhouette arcing gently across the skin of the sky. He closed his eyes. He was a young boy again, reclining with his brother to sleep in his mother's lap, the three of them waiting for his father's arrival, the weight of Pedro's bones settling to the ground now, one last time.

CHAPTER TWENTY-SIX

"¡Saturnina, Saturnina,
Bailarina de deseos clandestinos!
No rechases el impulso de lanzar
Al antojo especular.
No gastes tiempo zapateando con la inseguridad.
Lo que aparece no es fantasía pero verdad."

"*Ay, Tomás*, on a day like this, I can look up and see your face in the sky. My son."

She had brought every thread together, as her son wanted her to do. As for Armando and Conchita—Saturnina smiled gleefully. She had launched them all on a course together. As she approached the steps of the capitol, she could see the docents standing at the bottom of the steps, plump comrades, their well-fed bodies expanding through every button and seam of their uniforms.

"*Fidel calló,*" she called out to them factually, her ancient face as solid as stone. "*¡Fidel calló!* They found him and his brother dead in a puddle of blood. No one, nothing could save him, except of course our Lord and Savior. How the strongest of us fall away like an old building. Who could have known that such a thing could happen? How that ancient horse would fall like that. One step too many. His blood and ours. We all suffer with him, ladies. Don't you forget."

With each phrase, Saturnina lifted the ends of her voluminous skirts, pacing and turning before the steps of the capitol like an ancient chorus of one.

"*¡Viejita, silencio!*" one of the docents shouted.

"*Cayó y calló,*" Saturnina agreed. "He silenced and he fell. So much the old man had left to do, yet there he fell."

Saturnina pivoted and bowed low like an ancient ballerina, the tears streaming down her face as she remembered touching her son's wound.

"Come back to me," she called up to the sky. "The brothers are gone! Come back to me."

"Shut up! It's a stupid rumor," another docent called out.

"All those people out in the streets will pay for being so gullible," the docent of the greatest girth insisted.

Saturnina paid her no heed. She could see how her news had attracted the attention of a large group of German tourists.

"*¡Fidel cayó! ¡Fidel calló¡*" Saturnina called out to the tourists.

"*¡Estas loca, vieja!*" several docents shouted back in unison.

"Fidel silenced! Fidel fell!" Saturnina replied.

The urgency of her tone shook the docents' certainty, causing some of them to remember a long-dormant habit and form the shape of the cross in midair and all of them to begin trotting rapidly up the capitol's steps. The German tourists who witnessed this strange scene began leafing through their pocket dictionaries, patching together the meaning of Saturnina's words, pairing those words with the docents' reaction, and finding themselves before, not the gaudy street theater of a culture they considered both cipher and puerility, but a fragment of their own past, spent in the eastern portion of Berlin. The German tourists scurried back to the Hotel Nacional to pack their bags, to call home with the news, and to warn any other infelicitous travelers of the *golpe de estado*, the powerful stroke that had toppled the government, the debacle to which they had been indirectly privy.

Saturnina smiled up at the cloud of doves rising from the steps of the capitol into the late-afternoon sky and waved her little-girl wave at them.

"I'm already home." She wiped away her tears.

As she stood there in her terrible destitution, she knew this place was irrevocably hers. Homeless, childless, hungry, and half crazed, she was both exiled and completely ensconced, safe and certain of herself. She followed the arc of the birds' flight because really, if she continued to squint as she was doing now, they appeared to her as one giant dove whose wings gently embraced the warm air around her body, lifting her slightly off the ground.

She followed that gentle arc to the park in the center of the square near the Teatro García Lorca, skirting the edges of the milling crowd. There she found her old friend Martí standing, gleaming in white marble, his right hand extended, elbow slightly bent. It always seemed to her, whenever she looked up at him, that he was gently caressing the land he had defended with his life. Saturnina circled Martí's statue three times clockwise. Then, bowing deeply, her torso disappearing into the center of her bloodied skirts, three times counterclockwise she went until she came to stand before him.

Raising her right arm in a caress that mirrored his, she confided in him her favorite old joke:

"*Hasta aqui llega la mierda.* The shit's up to here, *¿eh, Poeta?*"

"*¡Socorro! ¡Socorro!*"

Saturnina heard the cry for help and turned just in time to see a gaunt old man running as fast as he could across the square, his pockets bulging, a string of bells around his neck, at his side two young women in white coats, one of them carrying a black bag.

"The danger has passed." Saturnina shrugged. "You have nothing to fear now."

Saturnina turned to face the statue of Martí again.

"*¡Poeta! ¡Fidel cayó y Fidel calló!* That ancient horse of a man fell, ending his life the way he began it, in a puddle of blood. Hard is the hand of fate that raises and then casts a man down, shoving him from a balcony in a shot, pushing him down while his brother stands there, grasping the air for support, maybe even feeling guilty. Poet, my poet, what will we do now? Yes, we are mules. Even if God's hand took our blinders off, we still couldn't see. Who is so faithless that he will not mourn the death of a man who fell like a horse, his little red legs turned up toward the sky? Who mourns, Poet, the man who ends his life in fear?"

The old men who usually lined the perimeter of the park, playing their afternoon game of dominoes well into the twilight, turned their eyes from the churning crowd to Saturnina, who appeared to them as a crone capable of bewitching them all. Their faces were so furrowed by time that it was hard to read their expressions. In that moment, Saturnina's conversation with Martí was theirs, too. They were part of this moment: the putrid feces of partially digested hopes and poisoned words rising, the tide pushing these corpse-men to the same watermark of memory. They were all remembering the same moment in January of '59, when the Horse had come down from the Sierra Maestra and into the city with the promise of righting every wrong. There they had stood, the stags of their generation, strong and virile, so tired of the torture and repression of Batista, of the U.S. colonial interventions that had left them bereft of constitution and government. They were twenty, twenty-five years old then, and what had they done?

"No llores como una mujer lo que no defendistes como un hombre!" Saturnina cackled at them, as if she could sense

their collective guilt, lifting the edges of her bloodied skirts and spinning playfully.

"Don't cry like a woman over what you never defended as a man."

They could feel the shadows of their young bodies, flesh and bone, twitching beneath the sinews they had decayed into now. They turned to look at one another for the first time in many years and saw not the ravaged carcasses that time had left strewn around the perimeter of the park but much younger men who held the sacred wafer of life on the tip of their common tongue.

"*¡Fidel calló!*" Saturnina bellowed at them.

He had indeed fallen. He had fallen upon them about a half century ago, and they had poured into the streets, most of them, to welcome the change, so tired were they of the injustice of what had preceded him. And when the dust began to settle, slowly, the streets became the only solace for a hungry belly, or any ache that could not be salved. There were no medicines, no anodynes of any sort, not an aspirin or an air conditioner that would soften the grip of old age, ameliorate its pains.

"*¡Fidel cayó! ¡Fidel calló!*"

The sound of the old woman's voice boomed over the chanting crowd, radiating outward to form a vortex of

invisible, concentric circles, G-forces of the spirit pressing in on them. Space and time seemed to enfold one
upon the other until, at that very moment, the brothers of
these old men, themselves old, sitting along the streets of
Calle Ocho in Miami, playing dominoes and champing
the ends of not-quite-Cuban cigars, felt the golden cur-
tain, the haze of that utopian diorama they referred to in
their daydreams as Cuba, the Cuba that had existed before Fidel, come away like the wrinkled skin on boiled
milk. What they saw at that moment was what they had
not been willing to see, these staunch conservers of a state
that had never really existed as they remembered it, for
the many decades of their exile.

For they, too, like their island-bound brothers, had run
out into the streets on that fateful January day in 1959,
and yes, yes, they had welcomed Fidel into the city with
the same fervor and hope as the peasants who sheltered
him in the mountains all those long months of civil war.
They had not been more prescient than their island-
bound brothers. They had been equally jubilant, and their
wives had run to the dressmakers to have their special
mambo dresses fitted for the public celebrations, those
endless streams of ruffles on those hyperbolic, cinched
rumps, forming their swaying bodies into an undulating

human version of the Cuban flag, red and white and blue, to welcome the descent of the Horse from the Sierra Maestra, to welcome the beginning of political self-determination.

"*¡Fidel cayó y Fidel calló y Tomás llego!*"

Space and time collapsed in the vortex of that dark Madonna's eye as she drew everyone into the silent circle formed between her eye and belly. Every one of those old men, on island and peninsula, slave of commune or capital, felt his life beginning and ending at that moment. Time had stopped; the revolution was complete. What Saturnina stirred in the hearts and loins of those old men, the collective clarity with which they looked up into the twilight sky and into each other's eyes and mouthed the words *Fidel calló,* was barely perceptible. But then, how is change gauged in a catatonic patient? A memory of possibility, the trace of a lingering desire can be as easily overlooked as the flicker of an eyelash, the shift of the tongue into the basin of a mouth.

"*¡Fidel calló! ¡Tomás llego!*"

Saturnina danced one last time around the statue of Martí, cackling like a witch over her cauldron. Then she stopped, startled by the thunderous rumble of military tanks that slowed to a halt before the crowd. The hatch of the lead tank opened, then a helmet and the torso of a soldier emerged.

"*¡Vayanse!*" the soldier bellowed. "Cease and go home!"

The artillery guns on the tanks began to move, someone inside the belly of each great mechanical beast calibrating the first volley. A heavy silence fell over the crowd. The old men along the park's perimeter began walking slowly toward the tanks, their bodies leaning heavily against their canes or a friendly arm, their hips made limber by the news that Fidel, an old man like them, had fallen and that something else, something different from anything they had ever known in their long lives, was giving birth to itself. They were doing now what they had not done in their youth.

"*¡El pueblo unido jamás sera vencido!*"

From the depth of the crowd, a single voice rang out, cleaving the silence.

"A people united shall never be divided!"

The crowd roared, its strength renewed. Saturnina looked to see Camilo rising from its midst, raised on the shoulders of Armando and a wiry old man who looked oddly familiar, and close behind them Conchita and Amparo, the latter holding a briefcase. Camilo's words had triggered a seismic shift, the formation of an immense wave of human will and conscience, that drew itself together, slowly surging forward until they surrounded the tanks, all the while chanting in one voice,

"*¡El pueblo unido jamás sera vencido!*"

"*¡El pueblo unido jamás sera vencido!*"

To Saturnina, the lead soldier seemed dazed, confused by the crowd's response. He took off his helmet as if to plead his case with them, and Saturnina smiled with glee. She pushed her way to the front of the crowd until she reached the side of the lead tank. She looked up at the young soldier's face, and he looked down at hers.

"*¿Que van hacer?*" she shouted at the soldier with the crooked smile. "What will you do?" she shouted. "Who will you stand with now? You gave me bread. You called me mother. We all know who you are, boy." Saturnina winked mischievously at the soldier. "What will you do now?"

The crowd continued to press forward, their chants cacophonous, deafening. The soldier with the crooked smile disappeared into the belly of the tank. An eternity seemed to pass, and then the crowd roared: The guns were swiveling away from them and the tanks beginning their slow crawl toward La Plaza de la Revolución, the mounting crest of the crowd behind them, pushing, guiding.

ACKNOWLEDGMENTS

★

Emerson, that great navigator of the human soul, observes with a certainty as quiet as it is adamantine that when we look back across the years "[t]he whole course of things goes to teach us faith." All we have to do is submit to the force that impels and guides us, delivering ourselves to "the full centre of that flood"—even when all we can see are the endless tacks that seem to lead nowhere and amount to nothing. At every moment when I was, at best, a very poor student of Emerson, I was given by grace the presence of extraordinary individuals who saw what I couldn't see and who, with their kindness and patience, their extraordinary intellects and heart, helped me navigate the next tack. There is no adequate way to thank them, but I will, with the deepest gratitude and respect, name them here: Marc Silverstein and Alice Grellner;

ACKNOWLEDGMENTS

William Keach and Richard Peabody; Wanda Needleman and Beverly Brosky; C.D. Wright and Michael Harper; Father Horace H. Grinnell and Sister Agustina Temprano; H. Keith Gold and M. Claudia Benassi; Linda Robinson and Mercia Ordman Rindler; Katie Grimm and Frederick Ramey. This course that is my life would be very different without you. There is a special cruelty about life in exile and the immorality of an embargo the putative target of which is material. There is, too, the response of the human heart that brooks neither cruelty nor immorality. Rolando and Yolanda Martínez; Rolandito and Juan Carlos Martínez; Miguel Martínez, the late Carmen Martínez Pérez, and the late Pedro Martínez: Your heroism is real, your love persists, endures, and transforms.